Christmas Morning

stories and poems

edited by Roswitha Classen

Ernst Klett Schulbuchverlag
Stuttgart Düsseldorf Berlin Leipzig

Herausgegeben von Roswitha Classen, Göttingen.

The cassette accompanying this book contains the stories by Frank O'Connor, B.J. Chute, Bernard Mac Laverty and Martha Brooks; the poems by Thomas Boyle and C. S. Lewis; and *Is There a Santa Claus ?* (anon.). Klett-Nummer 57749

Gedruckt auf Papier aus chlorfrei gebleichtem Zellstoff, säurefrei.

1. Auflage 1 5 4 3 2 1 | 1998 97 96 95 94
Alle Drucke dieser Auflage können im Unterricht nebeneinander benutzt werden. Die letzte Zahl bezeichnet das Jahr dieses Druckes.

Redaktion: Katherine Inglis-Meyer, M.A.

Umschlaggestaltung: Christa Janik, Stuttgart.
Druck: Wilhelm Röck, Weinsberg
Printed in Germany.
ISBN 3-12-577480-2

Contents

Introduction

This anthology is intended for senior pupils as well as for adult learners of English. At school it could create the right atmosphere in the last lessons before the Christmas holidays, but for all other lovers of English literature it is simply "A Present for Christmas".

The selection of short stories and poems has been compiled to show different ways of celebrating Christmas in the English-speaking world: in Britain, Ireland, the USA, Canada and even South Africa. Carol singing and church services commemorate the birth of Christ all over the Christian world. But where British or American influence prevails certain traditions have developed that differ from what we in Germany normally associate with Christmas.

The stories printed here illustrate some of these: Santa Claus comes to life in the editorial of *The New York Sun* as well as in the short story by the Irish writer Frank O'Connor. With Noël Mostert the reader can enjoy a fabulous Christmas dinner in South Africa featuring turkey, pies, Christmas pudding and crackers. B. J. Chute on the other hand, encourages reflection and provokes laughter on the subject of sending Christmas cards to almost everyone, while Chet Williamson mingles features from ghost stories and thrillers with a religious motif in his story about a Santa in an American supermarket. Northern Ireland is the scene of Bernard Mac Laverty's story about a poverty-stricken down-and-out who gets an unexpected Christmas present whereas Canada is the setting for Martha Brooks' perceptive tale of a teenager spending Christmas among old people for the first time in her life.

Should Christmas be celebrated as a social event, an occasion for being happy and showing good will to everyone, or is it rather something private, a family affair full of emotions and memories? Whichever the answer, there is in this collection ample material for discussion and comparison with Christmas customs in our country. But above all the stories are meant to be enjoyed, as befits the Christmas season.

For reasons of consistency all explanations are given in British English, and in the case of American texts, the differences between American and British spelling have been pointed out where necessary.

Is There a Santa Claus?

(The following article originally appeared on the editorial page of The New York Sun, *September 21, 1897, and was reprinted for many years in the December 24 editions of the newspaper.)*

We take pleasure in answering at once and thus prominently the communication below, expressing at the same time our great gratification that its faithful author is numbered among the friends of *The Sun:*

Dear Editor, I am 8 years old.
Some of my little friends say there is no Santa Claus.
Papa says "If you see it in *The Sun* it's so."
Please tell me the truth. Is there a Santa Claus?

Virginia O'Hanlon
115 West Ninety-fifth Street

Virginia, your little friends are wrong. They have been affected by the skepticism of a skeptical age. They do not believe except they see. They think that nothing can be which is not comprehensible by their little minds. All minds, Virginia, whether they be men's or children's, are little. In this great universe of ours man is a mere insect, an ant, in his intellect, as compared with the boundless world about him, as measured by the intelligence capable of grasping the whole of truth and knowledge.

Yes, Virginia, there is a Santa Claus. He exists as certainly as love and generosity and devotion exist, and you know that they abound and give to your life its highest beauty and joy. Alas! How dreary would be the world if there were no Santa Claus! It would be as dreary as if there were no Virginias. There would be no childlike faith then,

4 **prominent** ['---] noticeable – 5 **gratification** pleasure – 13 **affected** influenced – 15 **comprehensible** understandable – 17 **mere** word used to emphasize how small s.th. is – **ant** *Ameise* – 18 **boundless** without limits – 19 **to grasp** *here:* to understand – 22 **generosity** [ˌdʒenəˈrɒsətɪ] the quality of giving more than is expected – **devotion** great love and affection – **to abound** to exist in great quantities – 23 **dreary** [ˈdrɪərɪ] dull, gloomy

no poetry, no romance to make tolerable this existence. We should have no enjoyment, except in sense and sight. The eternal light with which childhood fills the world would be extinguished.

Not believe in Santa Claus! You might as well not believe in fairies! You might get your papa to hire men to watch in all the chimneys on Christmas Eve to catch Santa Claus, but even if they did not see Santa Claus coming down what would that prove? Nobody sees Santa Claus but that is no sign that there is no Santa Claus. The most real things in the world are those that neither children nor men can see. Did you ever see fairies dancing on the lawn? Of course not, but that's no proof that they are not there. Nobody can conceive or imagine all the wonders there are unseen and unseeable in the world.

You tear apart the baby's rattle and see what makes the noise inside, but there is a veil covering the unseen world which not the strongest man, not even the united strength of all the strongest men that ever lived, could tear apart. Only faith, fancy, poetry, love, romance, can push aside that curtain and view and picture the supernal beauty and glory beyond. Is it all real? Ah, Virginia, in all this world there is nothing else real and abiding.

No Santa Claus! Thank God! he lives, and he lives forever. A thousand years from now, Virginia, nay, ten times ten thousand years from now, he will continue to make glad the heart of childhood.

1 **tolerable** ['----] bearable – 3 **to extinguish** to put out – 11 **to conceive** to form an idea in one's mind – 14 **veil** *Schleier* – 16 **faith** belief – **fancy** *here:* imagination – 17 **supernal** *(lit.)* divine, godly – 19 **abiding** lasting – 21 **nay** *(lit.)* no

Frank O'Connor

Christmas Morning

Coming on to dawn, I woke with the feeling that something dreadful had happened. The whole house was quiet, and the little bedroom that looked out on the foot and a half of back yard was pitch-dark. It was only when I glanced at the window that I saw how all the silver had drained out of the sky. I jumped out of bed to feel my stocking, well knowing that the worst had happened. Santa had come while I was asleep, had gone away with an entirely false impression of me, because all he had left me was some sort of book, folded up, a pen and pencil, and a tuppenny bag of sweets. Not even Snakes-and-Ladders! For a while I was too stunned even to think. A fellow who was able to drive over rooftops and climb down chimneys without getting stuck – God, wouldn't you think he'd know better?

Then I began to wonder what that foxy boy, Sonny, had. I went to his side of the bed and felt his stocking. For all his spelling and sucking-up he hadn't done so much better, because, apart from a bag of sweets like mine, all Santa had left him was a pop-gun, one that fired a cork on a piece of string and which you could get in any huxter's shop for sixpence.

All the same, the fact remained that it was a gun, and a gun was better than a book any day of the week. The Dohertys had a gang, and the gang fought the Strawberry Lane kids who tried to play football on our road. That gun would be very useful to me in many ways, while it would be lost on Sonny who wouldn't be let play with the gang, even if he wanted to.

Then I got the inspiration, as it seemed to me, direct from heaven. Suppose I took the gun and gave Sonny the book! Sonny would never

1 **dawn** early morning just before sunrise – **dreadful** terrible – 3 **foot and a half** very small (one foot = 0.3 metres) – **pitch-dark** very dark – 4 **to glance** to look quickly – 5 **to drain out** to run out like water – 9 **tuppenny** two pennies or twopence, cheap – **Snakes-and-Ladders** popular game played with dice – 10 **stunned** shocked – 13 **foxy** clever (in a negative way) – 14 **to suck up** *(slang)* to try to please – 17 **huxter** or **huckster** *usu.* s.o. who sells things in the street, pedlar

be any good in the gang: he was fond of spelling, and a studious child like him could learn a lot of spellings from a book like mine. As he hadn't seen Santa any more than I had, what he hadn't seen wouldn't grieve him. I was doing no harm to anyone; in fact, if Sonny only knew, I was doing him a good turn which he might have cause to thank me for later. That was one thing I was always keen on, doing good turns. Perhaps this was Santa's intention the whole time and he had merely become confused between us. It was a mistake that might happen to anyone. So I put the book, the pencil, and the pen into Sonny's stocking and the popgun into my own, and returned to bed and slept again. As I say, in those days I had plenty of initiative.

It was Sonny who woke me, shaking me to tell me that Santa had come and left me a gun. I let on to be surprised and rather disappointed in the gun, and to divert his mind from it made him show me his picture book, and cracked it up to the skies.

As I knew, that kid was prepared to believe anything, and nothing would do him then but to take the presents in to show Father and Mother. This was a bad moment for me. After the way she had behaved about the langing [playing truant], I distrusted Mother, though I had the consolation of believing that the only person who could contradict me was now somewhere up by the North Pole. That gave me a certain confidence, so Sonny and I burst in with our presents, shouting: "Look what Santa Claus brought!"

Father and Mother woke, and Mother smiled, but only for an instant. As she looked at me her face changed. I knew that look; I knew it only too well. It was the same she had worn the day I came home from langing, when she said I had no word.

"Larry," she said in a low voice, "where did you get that gun?"

"Santa left it in my stocking, Mummy," I said, trying to put on an injured air, though it baffled me how she guessed that he hadn't. "He did, honest."

4 **to grieve** to make unhappy – 5 **to do s.o. a good turn** to help s.o. – 8 **merely** just, only – 13 **to let on to be** (*dialect*) to pretend to be – 14 **to divert** to turn to a different direction – 15 **to crack s.th. up** (*informal*) to praise s.th. highly – 17 **to do s.o.** (*informal*) to be enough for s.o. – 19 **to lang** (*dialect*)**/to play truant** to stay away from school – 20 **consolation** comforting feeling – **to contradict** [,--'-] to say s.th. against s.o. – 22 **confidence** belief that you can deal with a situation successfully – 27 **to have no word** *(dialect)* to be dishonest – 29 **injured** ['--] insulted, offended – 30 **to baffle** to puzzle

"You stole it from that poor child's stocking while he was asleep," she said, her voice quivering with indignation. "Larry, Larry, how could you be so mean?"

"Now, now, now," Father said deprecatingly, "'tis Christmas morning."

"Ah," she said with real passion, "it's easy it comes to you. Do you think I want my son to grow up a liar and a thief?"

"Ah, what thief, woman?" he said testily. "Have sense, can't you?" He was as cross if you interrupted him in his benevolent moods as if they were of the other sort, and this one was probably exacerbated by a feeling of guilt for his behaviour of the night before. "Here, Larry," he said, reaching out for the money on the bedside table, "here's sixpence for you and one for Sonny. Mind you don't lose it now!"

But I looked at Mother and saw what was in her eyes. I burst out crying, threw the popgun on the floor, and ran bawling out of the house before anyone on the road was awake. I rushed up the lane behind the house and threw myself on the wet grass.

I understood it all, and it was almost more than I could bear; that there was no Santa Claus, as the Dohertys said, only Mother trying to scrape together a few coppers from the housekeeping; that Father was mean and common and a drunkard, and that she had been relying on me to raise her out of the misery of the life she was leading. And I knew that the look in her eyes was the fear that, like my father, I should turn out to be mean and common and a drunkard.

2 **to quiver with indignation** to tremble with anger – 3 **mean** *here:* nasty, unkind – 4 **deprecating** ['----] disapproving, critical – 7 **testy** impatient and angry 8 **cross** annoyed – **benevolent** [-'---] kind and helpful – 9 **to exacerbate** [ek'sæsəbeɪt] to make worse – 14 **to bawl** [ɔ:] to cry loudly – 19 **to scrape together a few coppers** to save a few pennies with great difficulty

Biographical Note

Frank O'Connor (1903–66) is one of the most popular Irish short story writers. Born as Michael Francis O'Donovan in Cork, he received only a minimum of formal schooling as his family was very poor, but he developed an interest in literature and languages at a very early age. He first started writing in Irish and later produced many translations of Irish literature. He lived for ten years in the U.S.A., but returned home when he had a stroke in 1961. He is best known for his collections of realistic short stories such as Guests of the Nation *(1931),* Crab Apple Jelly *(1944) and* My Oedipus Complex *(1963).* An Only Child *(1961) and the unfinished* My Father's Son *(1968) are autobiographical.*

Thomas Boyle

Christmas to Me was Snow

Christmas to me
was snow
but it never snowed
it always rained
or was sunny.
Once it snowed
and that was Christmas.
But the turkey got burnt
and when you chewed it
Mum said "Do you like it?"
and you said "Yes"
and that was her Christmas.
Dad's was a cigar
or an ounce of St Bruno or new slippers.

Thomas Boyle was born in 1957 and sent this poem to the Daily Mirror *at the age of 14.*

14 **ounce** measure of weight (28.35 gr.) – **St. Bruno** a brand of pipe tobacco – **slippers** shoes worn only in the house

B. J. Chute

Merry Christmas to All

"George," said George's wife, "do you think we should take the Harrisons off our Christmas card list this year?"

George Leacock grunted pleasantly and, using the one-eighth of his mind which was not occupied with the evening paper, asked who in hell were the Harrisons?

Joan said, "You know – the people we met on board ship."

"That was five years ago," said George, invoking the statute of limitations.

"I know, but we're still exchanging cards."

"Why?" said George.

"Well, you have to," said his wife. "I mean, if people send you cards, you have to send cards to them."

"Why?" said George and vanished back into the day's news.

There was a silence, then Joan said "George," and the monosyllable was quite exquisitely edged with frost.

"Yes, dear?" said George alertly, feeling the draft.

"I do think you might be more cooperative," Joan told him. "I have to buy the Christmas cards, and I don't know how many to get."

"Couple of dozen, I should think."

Joan put down her fountain pen, turned away from the desk and looked at her husband, long and hard. He sensed dimly that he had said the wrong thing and amiably revised his estimate. "Three dozen?"

"Oh, really!" said Joan. "You know very well we need at least a hundred. – George dear, don't just sit there and stare."

He continued to stare. "We can't possibly send out a hundred cards," he informed her in tones of outrage. "We don't even know a

3 **to grunt** to make a low, rough sound (like a pig)– 7 **to invoke** *(formal)* to quote s.th. to help your argument – 13 **to vanish** to disappear – 16 **alertly** [-'--] paying full attention – **draft** (*BE* **draught**) a current of cool air – 21 **to sense** to feel – **dimly** vaguely – 22 **amiably** ['eɪmɪəblɪ] in a friendly manner – **estimate** ['---] calculation – 26 **outrage** ['aʊtreɪdʒ] *here:* anger and shock

hundred people." He then put down his newspaper portentously, rose and stalked over to the desk. "It's ridiculous," he said and held out his hand. "Here, let me see your list."

She handed it to him silently, a small book that said *Gifts and Cards* on the outside and bristled within like a pincushion, full of names and addresses, written down, written over and generally hen-tracked. "There!" said George triumphantly. "You can't read your own handwriting, and you've counted everybody twice."

"I can read it," said Joan.

"Well, then, there's just too many people listed. No wonder Christmas always exhausts you. You wear yourself out with this kind of nonsense, and then –"

"Christmas does not exhaust me," she said, "and anyway what do you want me to do? Send the cards out on the Fourth of July?"

"We don't have to send so many," said George. "It's pure commercialism. Christmas is the season of peace and good will, a time to remember a few old friends you don't see often and you care about. Personally, I can't even remember what the Harrisons looked like."

"They were both very tall and thin, and they kept rushing around the deck and playing shuffleboard."

George groaned. "I remember. Couldn't abide 'em." Cheered by their obvious expendability, he brightened. "It goes to prove what I said – the whole thing's ridiculous. I'd sooner send a Christmas card to our newsboy."

"We do," said Joan.

"Do what?"

"Send a card to our newsboy," said Joan gently, educating him. "Well, we don't send it exactly. We give it to him when he brings the paper the day before Christmas. With a dollar in it."

"That's a tip," said George vigorously. "You see how commercial the whole thing is?"

"It's not a tip, it's a gift," said Joan with some exasperation. "And it's not in the least commercial. I always try to get him a card with a

1 **portentous** ['   ] ominous, pompous – 2 **to stalk** to walk in a stiff, angry way – 5 **to bristle** [brɪsl] *here:* to be full of s.th. – 6 **hen-tracked** from **hen-tracks** unreadable handwriting – 11 **to wear o.s. out** to tire o.s. – 20 **shuffleboard** game played on the deck of a ship (*Beilkespiel*) – 21 **to abide** *here:* to bear, stand – 22 **expendability** fact of being unnecessary or unimportant – 30 **tip** extra payment for a service – **vigorously** energetically, hotly – 32 **exasperation** [ɪgˌzæspəˈreɪʃn] annoyance, irritation

cocker spaniel on it, because he's got a cocker spaniel. Last year," she observed, "it was practically impossible because all the cards were French poodles."

"Look," said George with eloquent calm, and pulled up a chair. "Look, dear, I'm not surprised you get worked up over this every year, but –"

"I don't get worked up, George. I only asked if you thought the Harrisons should stay on the list."

He ignored her and remained soothing. "The thing to do is just sit here quietly, the two of us, and cut this list right down to rock bottom. You have enough to do at Christmas time without buying cards, addressing them, mailing them –"

"Licking the envelopes," said Joan helpfully.

"Licking the envelopes," said George, "and so forth. You have enough to do without all that. Now, there are perhaps three dozen people at the most we want to send cards to, and the Harrisons aren't of them."

"I think we should leave them on the list," said Joan, deciding suddenly. "It might hurt their feelings not to hear from us. We don't want to hurt their feelings at Christmas time, do we?"

"When else can we hurt their feelings?" said George reasonably. "We don't have any contact with them the rest of the year. No, dear, I'm going to take them off the list. Under *H.*"

"They aren't under *H,* they're under *I.* We know a lot of *H's* and only two *I's,* so I used most of the *I* heading for the *H's.*" She shook her head. "George, I think we ought to leave them on. They'll decide we're angry with them."

"How can we possibly be angry with someone we never see?"

"That's just it," said Joan tenderheartedly. "If we saw them we could explain, but this way they'll brood."

"Suffering catfish!" said George and, finding the Harrisons as advertised under *I,* he crossed them off with one explosive stroke. He then settled back and began to riffle through the pages of the list like a tiger leafing thoughtfully through the underbrush.

9 **to soothe** to calm, to quieten (down) – 10 **rock bottom** the very end; a very low level – 29 **tenderhearted** gentle and full of understanding – 30 **to brood** to think about s.th. for a long time with feelings of bitterness – 31 **catfish** big fish *(Wels)* – **suffering catfish!** *(exclamation)* for goodness sake – 33 **to riffle** to turn over the pages of a book without reading – 34 **to leaf through s.th.** *usu.* to turn the pages of s.th.; *here:* to move carefully through s.th.

"George –" said Joan.

But George had pounced. "Butler!" he exclaimed. "Butler, Margaret and James. Now, there's a perfect example of the – the fallacy of the whole thing."

"I don't see why."

"Because we see Peggy and Jim at least twice a week, all year round, that's why. They'll drop in on Christmas Eve like they always do. Why send them a card? Why can't we just say Merry Christmas when we see them and leave it at that?"

"Oh, *George.*"

"What do you mean – oh, George? That's no answer."

"It is too," said Joan. "I go to a great deal of trouble every year to find an especially nice card for Peggy and Jim, and they always put it on their mantelpiece. I got a lovely one last year, and they stood it right in front of the clock." She then added firmly, "And we put their card to us on the bookcase, you know that perfectly well. Peggy always looks to see if it's there."

George gave an insufficiently guarded snort.

Joan frowned. "She doesn't look in an obvious sort of way, but I can tell." She then added carefully, "George, if there's something about Peggy and Jim that you don't like, I wish you'd be perfectly frank and tell me what it is so we can talk it over. Peggy's my oldest friend, and I wouldn't want to feel that you feel –"

"I never said –" said George.

"Well, you implied it," said Joan, "and I do think it's better in a thing like this to be absolutely open and above-board, because –"

"Look," said George, very quickly, "we'll leave the Butlers on the list," and plunged in several pages beyond the *B's* where he felt on firmer ground. "Mr. and Mrs. T. Grady. Who the devil are Mr. and Mrs. T. Grady? What's the *T* for?"

"Thomas, Terence, Theodore – I don't know. He was the carpenter who put our bookshelves in for us. Mrs. Grady is his wife. Naturally."

"Oh, naturally," said George dryly. "Joan, would it be too much to ask why we send a Christmas card to the carpenter?"

2 **to pounce** to make a sudden attack – 3 **fallacy** ['fæləsɪ] lack of logic or good sense (in an argument) – 7 **to drop in** to pay a casual visit – 14 **mantelpiece** shelf above a fireplace – 18 **guarded** *here:* careful not to show one's feelings – **snort** loud sound made by breathing through the nose – 19 **to frown** to draw one's eyebrows together when one is angry – 25 **to imply** to mean s.th. without saying it – 26 **above-board** honest and open – 28 **to plunge** [plʌndʒ] to jump into s.th.

"Well, we've been exchanging cards for years," Joan said pleasantly. "Don't you remember that Mr. Grady left one of his tools behind him when he finished the bookshelves? I don't know just what kind of tool it was – screwdriver, maybe? Maybe a hammer."

In a somewhat strained voice, George said that the identity of the tool was not germane to the discussion.

"No, it isn't, is it?" said Joan. "Well, anyway, I dropped him a note to let him know we had his tool, and it was just before Christmas so I thought we should wish them a merry Christmas and it seemed nicer somehow to use a Christmas card. And then, after he came and got the tool, they sent us a card to thank us for letting them know about it and to wish *us* a merry Christmas. I thought it was very friendly of them."

"And year after year, into eternity, we have to go on sending cards to the Gradys?" said George incredulously. "They've moved out of town, even."

"Well, I wouldn't have normally, darling, but they sent us a card the next Christmas and told us their son had finished his basic training and was coming home for the holidays, so of course we sent a card to say how pleased we were –"

"Arrh," said George.

"Weren't you pleased?" said Joan. "You just told me that the Christmas season is a time for good will."

George leaned his head on his hand. "Joan dear, naturally, it was the happiest hour of my life when Grady, junior – whom I would not know from Adam – finished his basic training. It was the hour for which I had waited all my life – No!" said George in a sort of smothered scream. "I do *not* care about Master Grady. He can be a major-general, and I still don't care."

"He's a technical sergeant," Joan said placidly, "and I think it's very nice. He's engaged too. Mrs. Grady said so, on last year's Christmas card. I expect they're married by now."

"We can send a Christmas card to the grandkiddies," said George with considerable bitterness. He looked at the *G* page again, and even

4 **screwdriver** a tool used to tighten screws – 5 **strained** tense, nervous – 6 **germane** *(formal)* [-'-] basically important, relevant – 14 **incredulous** [-'---] unbelieving – 20 **Arrh!** exclamation expressing annoyance – 26 **smothered** [ʌ] *here:* held back, covered up – 29 **technical sergeant** ['sɑ:dʒənt] middle-ranking non-officer in the US Air Force – **placidly** calmly – 30 **engaged** planning to get married

he could see that the Gradys were set in everlasting granite. Muttering to himself, he moved into the *M's*. "McIntyre, Mrs. Oliver. Never heard of her."

"Oh sweetie! She was your mother's old cook."

"McIntyre? She was not. Our cook was a Norwegian and her name was Paulsen." He smacked his fist down on the desk and injured himself, but he would not be sidetracked. "There you are, Joan, that's just the sort of thing I mean. Here you've been sending a card all these years to some outlandish character named McIntyre because you thought she was Mrs. Paulsen. High time this list got checked."

"She married again," said Joan calmly.

"She did nothing of the sort, she never – Oh," said George. After a moment, he added lamely, "So she did. Married a man named McIntyre. Well, well. Well, well, well." Whistling to himself in a nonchalant manner, he got out of the *M's* as gracefully as possible and sheltered in the *N's*. "Neilson," he said hastily. "Norman, Newcomb –"

"Maybe we should take the Newcombs off," Joan suggested. "He's not with your firm any more."

George looked at his wife, shocked and hurt by her callousness. "My dear girl, I wouldn't dream of taking old Bob Newcomb off our Christmas list. You have absolutely no sense of fitness, Joan. After what Bob Newcomb and I went through together in that Rogers deal, the least I can do at Christmas time is to send him my good wishes. My *best* wishes. Really, Joan, there are times when I don't understand you."

"No," said Joan meekly. "I suppose not."

"We send a card to Bailey, of course?"

"Bailey?"

"Frederick Bailey – the fellow who took Bob Newcomb's place."

"You never told me to send him a card," said Joan.

"Them, not him. He has a wife. You have to include the wife in greetings, dear," he said instructively, "it's only polite. Mr. and Mrs. Frederick Bailey, somewhere on Blake Avenue. I'll get the address for you. Nice chap, Bailey, but rather stupid." He reached over and took her pen. "Here, I'll write them in."

1 **to mutter** to say s.th. in a low voice – 6 **to smack** to hit hard – 7 **to sidetrack s.o.** to take s.o.'s attention away from the main problem or point – 9 **outlandish** strange – 14 **nonchalant** ['nɒnʃələnt] carefree, calm – 15 **gracefully** elegantly – 16 **to shelter** to find protection – 19 **callousness** ['   ] insensitivity, heartlessness – 22 **deal** *here*: an agreement made in business – 26 **meek** mild, gentle

"George –" said Joan.

He already had pen poised. "Very little room under the *B's,*" he announced crisply, after a brief survey. "I'll put the Baileys at the bottom of the *A's.* Anderson, Adams, Akers – Where's Peter Arnold? We certainly send a Christmas card to Pete Arnold, don't we?"

Joan laced her fingers together and supported her chin on them, the better to gaze at her husband. "Arnold?" she said gently.

"Sure. Pete – our elevator operator at the plant. Good Lord, dear, Pete's been there three, no, four years now. Always has a Christmas wreath in the elevator and a cheerful word for everybody. We certainly ought to send him a Christmas card, darling. It's most unfriendly not to."

"Is there," said Joan tenderly, "a Mrs. Arnold?"

"No, Pete never married." He wrote *Arnold, Peter,* on the list with affectionate zeal and smiled at Joan in the same spirit. "Put a nice friendly little thought on the card, won't you? Something warm and Christmasy. You know what I mean."

"Yes, dear, I know just what you mean," said Joan and gazed in meditation at her list.

Her husband glanced at his watch and whistled mildly. "Getting late." He got to his feet, stretching. "Well, there you are," he said brightly. "That wasn't much of a job now, was it? Rather pleasant actually – remembering old friends. Of course, that's what Christmas is for."

Full of contentment and Yuletide spirit, he went back to his armchair and newspaper and was halfway through a headline before he was struck by another useful thought. "You know, Joan," he said, "it seems to me it's a mistake for you to take the Harrisons off that list. It would be too bad to hurt their feelings. Especially," said George judiciously, "at Christmas time."

2 **poised** held ready to move – 3 **crisply** *here:* in a cool, business-like way – 6 **to lace together** to link – 7 **to gaze** to look at s.th. steadily and for a long time – 8 **plant** *here:* factory – 9 **Christmas wreath** fir branches bound together to form a ring (American variation of the German *Adventskranz*) – 15 **affectionate** loving – **zeal** eagerness – 25 **Yuletide** Christmas time – 29 **judicious** [dʒuːˈdɪʃəs] *(formal)* showing good sense and judgement

He gazed at her affectionately over the top of his newspaper. She seemed rather thoughtful, and being a sensitive man he understood why. Christmas lists rightly belonged in the wife's domain, and it might well be that she resented a little the efficiency with which he had taken charge.

Still, when things got out of control, someone had to take a firm stand. This year, for instance, he must really buy the Christmas tree himself, instead of leaving it to Joan. Last year's tree, like last year's Christmas card list, had been far too large.

2 **sensitive** *sensibel* – 3 **domain** [-'-] field, sphere – 4 **to resent s.th.** to feel bitter about s.th. – **to take charge** to take over the responsibility for s.th.

Biographical Note

B(eatrice) J(oy) Chute (1913–1987) was born in Minneapolis, USA, one of three sisters who all grew up to be writers. While working as a secretary in her father's firm and also in a New York Police programme for underprivileged children she first became known as a writer of children's books. Later she also published a number of successful novels for adults (e.g. The Fields are White, *1950;* Greenwillow, *1956, which was adapted for a Broadway musical; and* The Moon and the Thorn, *1961). B .J. Chute was President of the American branch of P.E.N. from 1951 to 1961, and as an established writer she taught creative writing at Barnard College, Columbia University. She also wrote two collections of very enjoyable short stories* (The Blue Cup and Other Stories, *1957, and* One Touch of Nature and Other Stories, *1965, from which the story reprinted here is taken).* Merry Christmas to All *is typical of Chute's way of depicting her characters with deep psychological insight and refreshing humour.*

Chet Williamson

O Come Little Children

"It even *smells* like Christmas," the boy told his mother, as they strolled down the narrow aisles of the farmer's market. That it looked and sounded like that happiest of holidays went without saying. Carols blared everywhere, from the tiniest of the stand-holder's transistor radios to the brass choir booming from the market's PA system. Meat cases were framed with strings of lights, a myriad of small trees adorned a myriad of counters across which bills the color of holly were pushed and goods and coins returned, and red and green predominated above all other hues. But it was the odors that entranced: the pungency of gingerbread, the sweet olfactory sting of fresh Christmas cookies. There were mince pies and pumpkin pudding, and a concoction of cranberry sauce and dried fruit in syrup whose aroma made the boy pucker and salivate as though a fresh lemon had brushed his tongue. The owner of the sandwich stand was selling small, one-dollar, Styrofoam plates of turkey and stuffing to those too rabid to wait until Christmas, three long days away. The smell was intoxicating, and the line was long.

The boy's mother, smiling and full of the spirit, bought many things that would find their way to their own Christmas table, and the sights

2 **aisle** [aɪl] *here:* passage between the rows of shelves or stands in a supermarket – 4 **to blare** to sound like a trumpet – 5 **brass** *here:* trumpets and other wind instruments – **to boom** to make a loud deep sound – **PA system** public-address system – 6 **myriad** ['mɪrɪəd] a very great number – 7 **to adorn** to decorate – 8 **to predominate** [-'---] *here:* to be most noticeable – 9 **hue** shade of a colour – **odor** ['--] (*BE* **odour**) smell – **to entrance** [-'-] to fill with wonder – 10 **pungency** ['pʌndʒənsɪ] sharp smell – **gingerbread** dark cake or biscuit flavoured with ginger *(Ingwer)* and other spices – **olfactory** [-'---] *(lit.)* relating to the sense of smell – 11 **mince pie** Christmas pie with spicy sweet filling – **pumpkin** *Kürbis* – **concoction** mixture – 12 **cranberry** *Preiselbeere* – 13 **to pucker** to press one's lips together – **to salivate** to have a watery mouth – 15 **stuffing** filling (of turkey, etc.) – **rabid** *here:* keen, eager – 16 **to intoxicate** [-'---] *here:* to make you excited

and sounds and smells kept the boy from being bored, as he usually was at the Great Tri-County Farmer's and Flea Market.

It was on the way out, as he and his mother walked through the large passage that divided the freshness of the food and produce stands from the dusty tawdriness of the flea market, that the boy saw the man dressed as Santa Claus. At first glance he did not seem a very *good* Santa Claus. He was too thin, and instead of a full, white, cottony, fake beard, his own wispy mass of facial hair had been half-heartedly lightened, as though he'd dipped a comb in white shoe polish and given it a few quick strokes. "There," the boy's mother remarked, "is one of Santa's *lesser* helpers."

The boy was way past the point where every Santa was the *real* Santa. In truth, he was just short of total disbelief. TV, comic books, and the remarks of older friends had all taken their toll, and he now thought that although the existence of the great man was conceivable, it was not likely, and to imagine that any of these kindly, red-suited men who smiled wearily in every department store and shopping mall was the genuine article was quite impossible.

Even if he had believed fully, he doubted if anyone under two would have accepted the legitimacy of the Santa he saw before him. Aside from the thinness of both beard and frame, the man's suit was threadbare in spots, the black vinyl boots scuffed and dull, and the white ruffs at collar and cuffs had yellowed to the color of old piano keys. His lap was empty. The only person nearby was a cowboy-hatted man sitting on a folding chair identical to that on which the Santa sat. A Polaroid Pronto hung from his neck, and next to him a card on an easel read YOUR PICTURE WITH SANTA – $3.00. The $3.00 part was printed much smaller than the words. The boy and his mother were nearly by the men when the one in the red suit looked at them.

2 **Tri-County** from three counties – 5 **tawdriness** from **tawdry** ['tɔ:drɪ] attractive but cheap and of bad quality – 7 **cottony** made of cottonwool *(Watte)* – 8 **fake** imitation – **wispy** thin and irregular – 11 **lesser** *(lit.)* not as great as others – 12 **way past** *(AE informal)* a long way beyond – 14 **to take its toll** *here:* to have a serious effect – 15 **conceivable** thinkable, imaginable – 17 **wearily** in a tired manner – **shopping mall** [mɔ:l] *(US)* shopping centre – 18 **genuine article** real thing – 20 **legitimacy** [lɪ'dʒɪtɪməsɪ] – 21 **frame** *here*: body – **threadbare** [θredbeə] worn out, thin – 22 **scuffed and dull** worn out and unpolished – 23 **ruff** *Krause, Rüsche* – **cuff** end of the sleeve at the wrist – 24 **lap** *Schoß* – 27 **easel** stand which supports a painting while the artist is working on it

The boy stopped. “Mom,” he said, loud enough for only his mother to hear. “May I sit on his lap?”

She gave an impatient sigh. “Oh, Alan …”

“Please?”

“Honey, do you really *want* your picture taken with ...?”

“I don’t want a picture. I just want to sit on his lap.”

“No, sweetie,” she said, looking at the man looking at the boy. “I don’t think so.”

They were in the parking lot by the time she looked at her son once more. To her amazement, huge tears were running down his face. “What’s wrong, honey?”

“I wanted to sit on his *lap*,” the boy choked out.

“Oh, Alan, he’s not Santa, he’s just a helper. And not a very good one either.”

“Can’t I? Please? Just for a minute…”

She sighed and smiled, thinking that it would do no harm, and that she was in no hurry. “All right. But no picture.”

The boy shook his head, and they went back inside. The man in the red suit smiled as he saw the boy approach without hesitation, and patted his thigh in an unspoken invitation for the boy to sit. The man in the cowboy hat stood up, but before he could bring the camera to eye level, the boy said, “No picture, please,” and the man, with a look of irritation directed at the boy’s mother, sat down again.

The boy remained on the man’s lap for less than a minute, talking so quietly that his mother could not hear. When he started to slide off, he stopped suddenly, as though caught, and his mother saw that the metal buckle of the boy’s loose-hanging coat belt had become entangled in the white plush of the man’s left cuff. The man tried unsuccessfully to extricate it with the fingers of his gloved right hand, then put the glove in his mouth and yanked his hand free. With his long, thin fingers he freed the boy, who hopped smiling onto the floor and waved a hand enclosed in his own varicolored mittens. When he rejoined his mother, he was surprised to find her scowling. “What’s wrong?”

5 **honey** *(AE informal)* affectionate form of address (cf. dear) – 9 **parking lot** *(AE)* car park – 12 **to choke out** *here:* to speak with difficulty – 20 **to pat** to tap gently with the open hand – **thigh** upper part of the leg – 27 **buckle** metal or plastic end of belt used to fasten it – **entangled** mixed up – 29 **to extricate** ['---] to free – 30 **to yank** to pull quickly – 32 **mittens** kind of gloves (with no separate parts for the four fingers) – 33 **to scowl** to have an angry expression on one’s face

"Nothing," she answered. "Let's go."

But he knew something was wrong and found out later at dinner. "*I* think he must have been *on* something."

"Oh, come on," his father said, taking a second baked potato. "Why?"

His mother went on as though he were not there. "He just *looked* it. He had these real hollow eyes, like he hadn't slept in days. Really thin. The suit just hung on him. And, uh ..." She looked at the boy, who pretended to be interested in pushing an unmelted piece of margarine around on his peas.

"What?"

"His hand. He took off his glove and his hand was all bruised, like he'd been shooting into it or something."

"Shooting what?" the boy asked.

"Drugs," his father said, before his mother could make something up.

"What's that? Like what?"

His mother smiled sardonically at his father. "Go ahead, Mr. Rogers. Explain."

"Well ... *drugs*. Like your baby aspirin, only a lot stronger. People take some drugs just to make them feel good, but then later they feel real bad, so you shouldn't ever take them at all."

"What's the shooting part?"

"Like a shot, when the doctor gives you a shot."

"Like Mommy's diabetes."

"Yeah, like that. Only people who take too many *bad* drugs have their veins ..." He saw the question on the boy's face. "... their little blood hoses inside their skin collapse on them. So they might stick the needles in their legs, or in the veins in the backs of their hands, or even their feet or the inside of their mouth, or ..."

"That's fine, thank you," his mother said sharply. "I think we've learned enough tonight."

"He wouldn't do *that*," the boy said. "He was too *nice*."

His father shook his head. "Aw, honey, you never know. Nice people can have problems too." And then his mother changed the subject.

3 **to be on something** to be taking drugs – 12 **bruised** [bru:ʒd] with black and blue marks as after an injury – 17 **sardonic** [-'--] laughing at s.o. else's difficulties – 23 **shot** *here:* injection – 24 **diabetes** [ˌdaɪə'bi:ti:z]

The next day the boy told his mother that he wished he could see Santa Claus again. "Santa Claus?" she asked.

"At the market. *You* know."

"Oh, Alan, *him*? Honey, you saw him yesterday. You told him what you wanted then, didn't you?"

"I don't want to tell him what I want. I just want to see him because he's *nice*. I *liked* him."

After the boy was in bed, his father and mother sat in the living room, neither of them paying attention to the movie on cable. "He say anything to you about Santa today?" he asked her.

She nodded. "Couple of times. You?"

"Yeah. He really went for this guy, huh?"

"I don't know why."

"Oh, Alan can be so compassionate – probably felt sorry for the guy."

She shook her head. "No, it wasn't like that. He really seemed drawn by him, almost as though ..." She paused.

"As though he really thought the guy was Santa Claus?" her husband finished.

"I don't know," she answered, looking at the car crash on the TV screen but not really seeing it. "Maybe."

She turned off the movie with no complaints from her husband, and began to go over the final list of ingredients for their Christmas dinner. "Uh-oh," she murmured, and went out to the kitchen. In a minute she returned, frowning lovingly at her husband. "Well, it's not that I don't appreciate your making dinner tonight, but I just realized your oyster stew used the oysters for the Christmas casserole."

"You're kidding."

"Nope." She was amused to see that there was actually panic in his face.

"What'll we *do*?"

"Do without."

"But ... but oyster casserole's a tradition."

"Some tradition – just because we had it last year."

12 **he went for this guy** *(AE informal)* he liked this man – 14 **compassionate** full of pity – 23 **ingredients** [ɪn'gri:djənts] different parts of a mixture – 25 **to frown** [fraʊn] to look at s.o. in a criticizing way – 26 **oyster** *Austern* – 27 **casserole** a dish you make by cooking food in liquid in the oven – 28 **to kid** *(informal)* to make a joke – 29 **Nope** *(informal)* no

"I liked it."

"And where are we going to find oysters on a Sunday?"

"It's not the day, it's the month. And December has an *R* in it."

"Sure. But Sunday doesn't have *oysters* in it. The IGA's closed, Acme, Weis … "

His face brightened. "The farmer's market! They have a fish stand, and they're open tomorrow. You could run out and … "

"Me? I didn't cook the oyster stew."

"You ate it."

She put her left hand over his head and pounded it gently with her right. "Sometimes you are a real sleazoid."

"Now, Mrs. Scrooge," he said, pulling her onto his lap, "where's that Christmas spirit, that charity?"

"Good King Wenceslas I ain't."

"How about if I vacuum while you're gone so my mother doesn't realize what a slob you are?"

"How many pounds of oysters do you want?"

It started to snow heavily just before midnight and stopped at dawn. The snow was light and powdery, easy for the early morning trucks to push from the roads. The family went to church, then came home for a simple lunch, as if afraid to ingest even a jot too much on the day before the great Christmas feast. "Well," the boy's mother said after they'd finished cleaning up the dishes, "I'm off for oysters. Anyone want to come?"

"To the farm market?" asked the boy. His mother nodded. "Can I see Santa?"

His father and mother exchanged looks. "I don't think so," she replied. "Do you want to go anyway?"

He thought for a moment. "Okay."

The parking lot was still covered with snow, although the cars had mashed most of it down to a dirty gray film. Only the far end of the

3 **December has an R in it** shellfish should be eaten in months with an *R* – 4 **IGA, Acme, Weis** big supermarkets in USA – 10 **to pound** to hit again and again – 11 **sleazoid** ['sli:zɔɪd] *(AE slang)* a mean person – 12 **Mrs Scrooge** allusion to Mr Scrooge, a very mean character in Dickens' *Christmas Carol* – 13 **charity** *here:* kindness and helpfulness – 14 **Good King Wenceslas** person in well-known Christmas carol who helps a poor man on St. Stephen's Day – 16 **slob** *(slang)* untidy person – 21 **to ingest** [ɪn'dʒest] *(lit.)* to eat – **jot** very small amount – 31 **to mash** to press

parking lot, where a small, gray trailer sat attached to an old, nondescript sedan, was pristine with whiteness. It was typical, the boy's mother thought, of the management not to pay to have the lot plowed – anyone who'd hire a bargain basement Santa like that one and then charge three bucks for a thirty-five cent picture with him.

The seafood stand was out of oysters, but its owner said that the small grocery shop at the market's other end might still have some. "Could I see Santa?" the boy asked as they walked.

"Alan, I told you no. Besides, he's probably gone by now. He's got a busy night tonight." She knew it sounded absurd even as she said it. If *that* Santa was going to be busy, it wouldn't be delivering toys – it would probably be looking for a fix. Repulsion crossed her face as she thought again of those hollow eyes, that pale skin, the telltale bruises on his bare hand, and she wondered what her son could possibly see in that haggard countenance.

She thought she would ask him, but when she looked down, he was gone. In a sharp, reflexive motion, she looked to the other side, then behind her, but the boy was not there. She strained to see him through the forest of people, then turned and retraced her steps, as her heart beat faster and beads of cold sweat touched her face. "Alan!" she called, softly but high, to pierce the low, murmuring din around her. "Alan!"

It took some time for the idea to occur that her son had disobeyed her and had set out to find the market's Santa Claus on his own. She had not thought him capable of such a thing, for he knew and understood the dangers that could face a small child alone in a public place, especially a place like a flea market that had more than its share of transients and lowlifes. She told herself that he would be all right, that nothing could happen to a little boy the day before Christmas, that someone she knew would see him and stop him and take care of him

1 **trailer** *here:* caravan – **nondescript** uninteresting in appearance – 2 **sedan** [-ˈ-] *(AE)* car with seats for four or more people with a fixed roof – **pristine** [ˈprɪstaɪn] *(lit.)* extremely clean or new – 3 **to plow** (*BE* **to plough**) *here:* to sweep clear of snow – 5 **to charge** *here:* to ask for payment – **buck** *(AE informal)* dollar – 12 **repulsion** *(formal)* a strong feeling of dislike and disgust – 13 **telltale** revealing – 15 **haggard** looking very tired and worried – **countenance** *(formal)* face – 18 **to strain** *here :* to try hard –19 **to retrace one's steps** to go back the same way –21 **to pierce** to get through – **din** noise – 28 **transient** [ˈtrænzɪənt] *here:* a drifter – **lowlifes** *(AE)* people who have low standards of morality

until she could find him, or that he would be there on Santa Claus's lap, smiling sheepishly and guiltily when he spotted her.

She was running now, jostling shoppers, their arms loaded with last-minute thoughts. Within a minute, she entered the large open area between the markets. The chairs and the sign were there, the Santa and his photographer were not. Neither was her son.

For a long moment she stood, wondering what to do next, and finally decided to find the manager and ask him to make an announcement on the PA system. But first she called her husband, for she could no longer bear to be alone.

By the time he met her in the manager's office, the announcement had been made four times without a response. The boy's father held his mother, who was by this time crying quietly, very much afraid. "Where was he going?" the manager, a short, elderly man with a cigarette in one hand and a can of soda in the other, asked.

"I thought it was to see Santa, but he wasn't there when I got there."

The manager nodded. "Yeah, he quit at noon. I wanted him to work through five, but he wouldn't. Said he hadda meet somebody."

The boy's father looked at the manager intently over his wife's head. "Who is this guy?"

"Santa? Don't know his name. Just breezed in about a week ago and asked if I wanted a Santa cheap."

"What do you mean you don't know his name? You *pay* him, don't you?"

"Cash. Off the books. You'll keep that quiet now. And Riley, my helper, he got a Polaroid, so we made enough to pay him outta the pictures."

The boy's father took his arms from around his wife. "Where is this guy?"

"He's got a trailer the other side of the lot."

"All right," the father nodded. "We're going to talk to him. And if he can't give us any answers, we're calling the police."

The manager started to protest, but the couple walked out of the office and down the aisles, trying hard not to run and so admit their

2 **sheepishly** in a slightly embarrassed way – **to spot** *here:* to see – 3 **to jostle** to bump against s.o. – 18 **he hadda** *(AE informal)* he had to – 19 **intently** [-'--] in a concentrated, attentive manner – 21 **to breeze in** *(informal)* to come in suddenly – 25 **off the books** the man is not in the official list of employees (for tax reasons etc.) – 26 **outta** *(AE informal)* out of

panic to themselves. "It'll be all right," the boy's father kept saying. "We'll find him. It'll be all right."

And they did. When they walked into the open area where Santa had been, their son was standing beside the gold aluminum Christmas tree. He smiled when he saw them, and waved.

They ran to him, and his mother scooped him up and hugged him, crying. His father placed a hand on his head as if to be certain he was really there, then tousled his hair, swallowing heavily to rid his throat of the cold lump that had been there since his wife's call.

"Where *were* you?" the boy's mother said, holding him ferociously. "Where did you *go?*"

"I wanted to see him," he said, as if that were all the explanation necessary.

"But I told you *no*. You know better, Alan. Anything could've happened. We were worried sick."

"I'm sorry, Mom. I just *had* to see him."

"But you didn't," his father said. "So where *were* you? Why didn't you answer the announcements?"

"Oh, I saw him, Dad. I was *with* him."

"You ... *where?*"

"He was here. He said he was waiting for me, that he'd been hoping I'd come again. He looked really different, he didn't have on his red suit or anything."

His mother shook her head. "But ... I *looked here.*"

"Oh, I *found* him here okay. But then we went to his place."

"*What?*" they both asked at once.

"His trailer. It's sort of like the one Grandpa and Grandma have."

"Why ... did you go out there?" his mother asked, remembering the trailer and the car at the end of the lot.

"He asked me to."

"Alan," his father said, "I've told you never, *never* to go with anyone for *any* reason."

"But it was all right with him, Dad. I knew I'd be safe with *him*. He told me when we were walking. Out to his trailer."

"Told you *what?*"

"How he always looks for somebody."

6 **to scoop up** to lift – **to hug** to hold s.o. tightly and lovingly in one's arms – 8 **to tousle** ['taʊzl] *here:* to stroke his hair making it untidy – 10 **ferocious** [fə'rəʊʃəs] fierce, violent

"Oh, my God. ... "

"What's the matter, Mom?"

"Nothing. Nothing. What else did this ... man say?"

"He just said he always comes back this time of year, just to see if people still believe in him. He said lots of people *say* they do, but they don't, not really. He said they just say so because they want their *kids* to believe in him. But if he finds one person who really believes, and knows who he really is, then it's all gonna be okay. 'Til next Christmas. He said it's almost always kids, like me, but that that's okay. As long as there's somebody who believes in him and trusts him enough to go with him."

The boy's father knelt beside him and put his big hands on the boy's thin shoulders. "Alan. Did he touch you? Touch you anywhere at all?"

"Just here," he held up his mitten-covered hands. "My hands."

"Alan, this man played a mean joke on you. He let you think that he's somebody that he really isn't."

"Oh no, Dad, you're wrong."

"Now listen. This man was *not* Santa Claus, Alan."

The boy laughed. "*I know that!* I haven't believed in Santa Claus for almost a whole *month!*"

His mother barely got the words out. "Then who ...?"

"And you were wrong too, Mom. He didn't have any little needle holes in his hands. Just the big ones. Straight through. Just like he's supposed to."

Her eyes widened, and she put her fist to her mouth to hold in a scream. Her husband leaped to his feet, his face even paler than before. "Where's this trailer?" he asked in a voice whose coldness frightened the boy.

They strode out the door together into the late afternoon darkness. Street lights illuminated every part of the parking lot. "It ... was there," she said, staring across at white emptiness.

"The *bastard.* Got out while the getting was good. He ..." The father paused. "There?" he said, pointing.

"Yes. It was right over there." The boy nodded in agreement with his mother.

8 **gonna be** *(AE informal)* going to be – 33 **bastard** ['--] *(vulgar)* a horrible person – **while the getting was good** while he could do so without getting into trouble

"It couldn't've been." He started to walk toward the open space, and his family followed. "There are no tracks. It hasn't snowed. And there's no wind." He looked at the unbroken plain of powdered snow.

"Hey! Hey, you folks!" They turned and saw the manager laboring toward them, puffs of condensation roaring from his mouth. "That your kid? He okay?"

The boy's father nodded. "Yeah. He seems to be. We were trying to find that man. Your Santa Claus. But he's ... gone."

"Huh! You believe that? And I still owe him fourteen bucks." He turned back toward the warmth of the market, shaking his head. "Left without his money. Some people ..."

"Never mind," his wife said. "He's all right. Let him believe." She touched her husband's shoulder. "Maybe we should all believe. It's almost easier that way."

When they got home, the boy took off his mittens, and his father and mother saw the pale red marks, one in each palm, where he said the man's fingers had touched him. They were suffused with a rosy glow, as if the blood pulsed more strongly there. "They'll go away," the boy's father said. "In time, they'll go away." But they did not.

2 **tracks** marks, traces – 4 **to labor** (*BE* **to labour**) *here:* to run with difficulty – 5 **puff** small cloud – 16 **palm** inner surface of the hand – 17 **suffused** [sə'fju:zd] filled or covered with s.th. – 18 **glow** [əʊ] brightness

Biographical Note

Chet Williamson, born 1945, is an American writer of thrillers, ghost stories and novels. His works include McKain's Dilemma *(1988),* Ash Wednesday *(1988) and* Dark Harvest *(1990).* O Come Little Children *was written in 1989 and appeared in an anthology called* Spirits of Christmas, Twenty Other-Worldly Tales. *Although the story is told in a very realistic way the reader wonders in the end if it is a fairy tale or an illustration of some of Jesus' words as related in Matthew 19, verses 13–15, and Matthew 25, verses 31–46.*

C. S. Lewis

The Nativity

Among the oxen (like an ox I'm slow)
I see a glory in the stable grow
Which, with the ox's dullness might at length
Give me an ox's strength.

Among the asses (stubborn I as they)
I see my Saviour where I looked for hay;
So may my beastlike folly learn at least
The patience of a beast.

Among the sheep (I like a sheep have strayed)
I watch the manger where my Lord is laid;
Oh that my baa-ing nature would win thence
Some woolly innocence!

Nativity [-'---] the birth of Christ – 2 **glory** great beauty – **stable** building where animals are kept – 3 **dullness** *here:* slowness in understanding – 5 **ass** donkey – **stubborn** unwilling to change one's mind – 6 **Saviour** Jesus Christ (= s.o. who saves) – 7 **beastlike** like an animal – **folly** foolishness – 9 **to stray** to wander away from the right path – 10 **manger** ['meɪndʒə] feeding box in a stable – 11 **to baa** to call like a sheep – **thence** *(lit.)* from there – 12 **innocence** ['ɪnəsəns] *opp. of* guilt, knowledge of evil

Biographical Note

C(live) S(taples) Lewis (1898–1963) was a literary critic and theologian as well as a writer of science fiction and children's literature. He was born in Belfast but educated mainly in England, becoming a Fellow of Magdalen College, Oxford in 1925 and Professor of Medieval and Renaissance English at Cambridge in 1955. His first collection of poems was published in 1918. About 1930 he was converted back to Christianity, an experience he describes in his spiritual autobiography Surprised by Joy *(1955). His radio talks on Christianity during World War II brought him wide popularity, as did the seven 'Narnia' stories for children which began with* The Lion, the Witch and the Wardrobe *(1950).The poem quoted here was published in 1964.*

Noël Mostert

A Christmas Dinner

Lyle began to feel about Christmas that he was permanently lost somewhere in the long passage between the kitchen and the dining room of his Aunt Anna's house, pivoting there with awkward gestures and murmurs of embarrassment, always standing aside for the purposes of others, for the trays of pineapple salad, cold duck and turkey, nuts and raisins, that went to the front, and the loads of glasses and silver and other things for cleaning that came out.

There seemed nowhere else to go; he was less in the way in the passage than in the dining room or kitchen, where the prevailing urgency spelled unmistakable exclusion. He felt in both of those places that true isolation of the outsider, of not knowing where things were, of being unable to respond to the constant exclamations for the objects that were missing or suddenly required.

It was eleven and he had been in the house for over an hour already. This dejected floating between other people's preoccupations was the logical anti-climax, it now seemed, to the unreal journey from Tokai reformatory; all the way out here through Capetown he had traveled blinking and self-conscious, as if the bright sunlight in which he worked shirtless every day were something as new and unfamiliar as his blue suit and tie. But the sense of the South African sun and the cool stillness before the heat of the day *was* different when he set out, though its quality and dove-laden murmur was indistinguishable in mood and modulation from all other days. Undoubtedly his being outside the gates made a difference in the mountains and in the surrounding vineyards and the pine forests he was used to, and he

3 **to pivot** to turn round and round on a central point – 9 **prevailing** predominant – **urgency** ['ɜːdʒənsɪ] *Dringlichkeit* – 10 **to spell** *here:* to mean – 13 **to require** [rɪ'kwaɪə] to need – 15 **dejected** [-'--] unhappy, depressed – 17 **reformatory** [-'---] educational institution for young criminals – 18 **to blink** to shut your eyes and then open them very quickly again – **self-conscious** embarrassed and nervous – 22 **dove-laden** filled with the sounds of pigeons *(Tauben)* – **indistinguishable** [--'---] similar, not different from s.th. else – 23 **modulation** tone, sound – 25 **vineyard** ['vɪnjəd] area of land planted with grapes for wine-making

decided that it was the sound of his footsteps unaccompanied on the dusty road toward the bus stop, the absence of any voices around him; the heaviness of the impending heat was sweet and languid instead of tense. But it was too still.

He went through a world in which everything seemed somewhere else; the people were busy with the special ceremonial of this day, and they were busy on their own.

"Merry Christmas," the bus conductor said offhandedly, and this made Lyle feel less timid and intrusive.

The bus was as empty as the road it traveled but there were colored-paper decorations inside to also remind him that it was Christmas. These, although dirty and torn, did not seem as perfunctory as those above the silent, watchful meals at the school, so that he went on with a mingled sense of skepticism and expectation; afraid of the unfamiliar, of the heavy responsibility of being alone and for every gesture he made and syllable he uttered.

When he'd left and gone out through the main hall, past the principal's office, Mr. Hendriks had called him in.

The principal was dressed as he normally was on a Sunday, in khaki shorts and with a short-sleeved open-neck shirt, and he was sucking a pipe. His two small daughters were there with him, nursing new dolls. Mr. Hendriks was a lean and athletic man; his eyes were sharp and flat as a detective's and he talked with the same sinister matter-of-factness, but he was not an unkind man. "You're going to behave yourself, aren't you?"

"Yes, sir."

"The last time you got probation you didn't." Mr. Hendriks was studying him carefully. He wasn't accusing or doubting, just recalling a fact which seemed to have some relevance. "Your relatives are good people. I know their minister. You know, it was good of your aunt to phone and ask for you. So you mus' jus' behave yourself, man. Jus' behave yourself and have a good time."

2 **absence** ['--] *opp. of* presence – 3 **impending** which is about to happen – **languid** ['læŋgwɪd] without energy – 8 **offhanded** showing little interest – 9 **intrusive** *here:* unwelcome – 12 **perfunctory** [-'---] done as a matter of routine – 14 **mingled** mixed – 17 **principal** *here:* headmaster – 21 **to nurse** *here:* to hold lovingly – 23 **sinister** ['---] frightening – 27 **probation** *here:* a test period of absence from prison – 29 **relatives** members of the wider family – 30 **minister** ['---] Protestant clergyman

"Yes, sir."

The strain of his fears that somehow he wouldn't, already had given him a slight headache and Lyle decided to leave the corridor and go outside. He went onto the verandah, but here too he was in the way, awkwardly on the fringe of the boisterous greeting incoming guests got as they burst through the small front gate, with gifts held high in arms outstretched for exultant embrace.

Lyle went inside again, found a chair in a darkened corner of the hall and sat holding his head in his hands, gazing at the floor and the frayed carpet with its design of camels and rampant lions.

"Is anything the matter, Lyle?" His Aunt Anna had approached him unaware and he jumped quickly to his feet.

"No," he said.

"Are you enjoying yourself?"

"Oh yes, thank you."

"Well, I'm glad they let you come. We very much wanted to have you. I don't suppose it's very nice staying there."

"No."

She regarded him intently. "Do they ... do they bully you much?"

"No."

"The man I spoke to, the principal, he seemed very nice. He said you've done very well lately and that you've been very good. Very quiet. That's why they let you come today. He said you're going out to St. Michael's home next month. Then you can go to trade school in the day."

"Yes."

"What are they going to teach you?"

"Electrician."

"Would you like that?"

"I don't know; I suppose so."

"Is there anything special you'd like to do now?"

"Have you got any books?"

She hesitated. "Well, we've got some nice books here you can look at, if you want to. Your uncle bought the *Encyclopaedia Britannica*. It's in the front, but be sure to wash your hands first. Do you read a lot there?"

2 **strain** state of worry and tension – 5 **fringe** edge – **boisterous** noisy and cheerful – 7 **exultant** joyous, triumphant – 10 **frayed** worn-out – **rampant** on their hind legs – 12 **unaware** without his noticing – 19 **to bully** [ʊ] to hurt and frighten s.o. weaker

"They don't have many books."

"You must make yourself at home; we're one happy family here."

"Oh, I do feel at home, thank you."

"Good." The word was a crisp satisfaction with duty done but something else occurred to her. "We'd have liked to have had you here instead of going to the home, of course. But we don't have so much room. You'll be free to come and visit us on Sundays though."

"Thank you very much, that'll be nice."

"Oh ... Heavens! Where do you people come from so suddenly?" She had turned to greet a raucous invasion.

There was momentary bedlam. Lyle drifted behind them into the kitchen, where one of the new arrivals, a woman in black Sunday best and pearls, was dancing excitedly from one foot to the other, and then cried to Anna, "Here let's give you a hand. We'll wash up and let Minnie get on with what she's doing." Minnie, the Malay maid, was standing scowling at the sink.

"No. You go inside. But come see this pudding first."

"It's beautifully done. You're so good at puddings. Mine never come out."

"I don't know what I'm doing anymore, what with everything." She gave Lyle an involuntary glance and was immediately embarrassed. The other woman looked as well.

"Is this Mary's boy?" she cried in the same, sharp voice. "Are you Jimmy? But you've grown! My God." Jimmy was Anna's grandchild.

"No," Anna said. "This is my nephew, Lyle. He's Julia's son. You remember Julia? Lyle's come for the day." She swallowed some further explanation and then called across the kitchen, "Lyle, get Auntie the cake forks, please. You'll find them in the dining room, in the sideboard."

He went with a rush, as though success or failure of the elaborate preparations in that hot, hissing, and littered kitchen, aglow with livid copper, split fruit, colored tarts, creams, and icings, were dependent upon imminent arrival of the forks.

4 **crisp** *here:* quick, precise, dry – 10 **raucous** ['rɔ:kəs] loud, noisy – 11 **bedlam** chaos – 16 **to scowl** to have an angry expression on your face – 21 **involuntary** [-'---] *ungewollt* – 26 **to swallow** *here:* to keep back – 30 **elaborate** [-'---] complicated – 31 **hissing** noisy with the sounds of cooking – **littered** untidy – **aglow** [ə'gləʊ] shining – **livid** *here:* dark red – 32 **icing** *Zuckerguß* – 33 **imminent** ['---] which will happen soon

An older cousin was standing on a chair in the dining room hanging decorations.

He began opening the sideboard drawers and she paused, holding a mass of red streamers which looped out from the ceiling centerpiece, a great scarlet paper bell. "What are you looking for?" she asked sharply.

"Auntie Anna wants the cake forks."

"Oh. They're in the top drawer there. No, the other one. Not those. Yes, those."

She watched him until he had taken the forks out, closed the drawer and started for the door.

He was about to rush back down the corridor when a familiar instinct stopped his pace and set his heart beating. He knew they were talking about him at the end. He went down the corridor casually, but skillfully silent. He stood quietly outside the kitchen door. Their voices retreated toward the oven, strengthened back to the center of the room.

"But where's the father?"

"God knows. Not that anyone cares."

"And Julia?"

"In Johannesburg, last I heard. I didn't ask him, but I don't think he knows either. I don't honestly want to know myself anymore where she or any of them are. It's your own flesh and blood but there's a limit."

"You've done very well, I think. It was good of you to have him today."

"The man at the reformatory called and asked us to have him – I don't know how he knew about us. Those people always seem to know things. So of course I said yes. One couldn't very well refuse, could one? He said they wanted to let him out of there next month and that the outing would do him good."

"Yes, but ..."

The conversation dropped to whispers.

Lyle entered. "Here are the forks," he said.

"Oh thank you, Lyle," Anna beamed, and the other woman smiled, her eyes going to and fro across his face, as if to read some story there.

4 **streamer** long paper ribbon – **to loop** to curve – 13 **pace** step – 14 **casually** ['kæzjʊəlɪ] in a relaxed manner – 15 **skillfully** (*BE* **skilfully**) cleverly – 31 **outing** little excursion – 35 **to beam** *here:* to smile cheerfully

Lyle said, "Excuse me, please," and went out into the hall. He felt a taste of sickness in his mouth.

The children were moving into the house and they went solemnly past him; they were coming from some point in the garden, where they had been hovering distractedly, restrained by their party clothes and absorbed in the malice of their various comparisons, one's toys against another's.

They entered in clusters, squeezing through the door, and with their quick movements and laughter they shook loose from their shoulders and shining hair the fragments of sunlight that still lay upon them, like bits of golden straw. They were all much younger than Lyle and they ignored him for this, also for that instinctive refusal in the community of the very young of association with the lost or isolated. He both envied and resented them; they wore the confidence of all the liberties conceded them that day.

The children had not been summoned, but a sure sense of the order and ritual of the occasion now brought them forward. An army of small masters, they advanced upon the lounge to exercise their prerogatives.

The tree was there of course. They moved unerringly to the various knees and laps that awaited them, and when they had settled, silent beneath the hubbub overhead, they fixed their attention upon the tree, scanning its base for new deposits from the late arrivals.

There was a mound of new stuff, all of it lavishly wrapped, and the room's ambrosial mist, a fragrance of Eau de Cologne, lavender, candle wax, mince pies and cigars, resin, new clothes and unbroken shoe leather, and brilliantine, seemed to emanate from there.

3 **solemnly** in a serious or grave manner – 5 **to hover** [ɒ] *here:* to wait in one place – **distractedly** in an unconcentrated way – **to restrain** to keep back, to hinder – 6 **malice** ['mælɪs] nastiness – 8 **cluster** small close group – 14 **to resent s.o.** [-'-] to feel bitter about s.o. – 15 **to concede** to allow – 16 **to summon** to ask formally to come – 18 **prerogative** [-'---] special privilege – 20 **unerringly** straight, without making a mistake – 21 **lap** *Schoß* – 22 **hubbub** noise of many voices – 23 **to scan** to look at s.th. carefully – 24 **mound** small hill, pile – **lavishly** *here:* expensively – 25 **ambrosial** *(lit.)* with a delightful smell (ambrosia = the food of the gods) – **fragrance** good smell – 26 **mince pie** small Christmas pie made with dried fruit and spices – **resin** ['rezɪn] sticky aromatic substance coming from pine and fir trees – 27 **to emanate** ['---] to come from s.o. or s.th.

Corks popped and each bottle apparently contained a gust of imprisoned laughter that burst into the room, foamed joyously around the walls, and then was reflectively amber.

"I shouldn't really."

"It's Christmas, what the hell. Just say when."

"Oh that's fine, thank you."

"How about you people?"

"Fill 'em up. Fill 'em up."

"They can say what they like, this is as good as French champagne any day."

"Good old South Africa."

Another round of gift-giving began for the children, who went forward like victors and returned with expressions of vanity and smug triumph to parental fuss.

Lyle retreated into his corner. Anna earlier had given him a pullover and a box of handkerchiefs but he felt now that he should be out of sight, that there was some obligation to avoid touching their conscience with this round, especially since the older children were going up as well. The distribution was soon over, however, and no one had noticed him. There was great hilarity.

Anna entered with a tray of gingerbeer for the children. She served them all and was about to leave when someone near Lyle called out, "You've missed somebody."

"Oh, I didn't see you there, Lyle," she said, with genuine concern. "Would you like some too?"

"Of course he does. Too young for champagne."

The glass came across. The room seemed heavily silent as he accepted it, without looking at anyone.

"Lyle's going to trade school soon; he's going to be an electrician," Anna said, to no apparent purpose, but as though in apology to Lyle.

Various people said, "Hmmm," or "Really?" and smiled in Lyle's direction. All the children turned to stare, examining him gravely, as

1 **gust** outburst – 3 **amber** golden coloured – 5 **say when** say when you have enough in your glass – 13 **vanity** pride – **smug** self-satisfied – 14 **to make a fuss of s.o.** to pay a lot of attention to s.o. – 20 **hilarity** [-'---] noisy happiness – 21 **gingerbeer** fizzy drink, usually non-alcoholic, flavoured with ginger *(Ingwer)* – 24 **genuine** ['dʒenjʊɪn] real, authentic – **concern** [-'-] *here: Sorge* – 30 **to no apparent purpose** without any clear aim or intention – **in apology** [ə'pɒlədʒɪ] as a way of saying 'sorry'

though there were some extra qualification for attention which they had somehow omitted from their own calculations for the day.

"That's a good trade. You'll make good money when you're qualified," one man said seriously, with that solemn tone used in addressing boys on a man-to-man basis. There were further murmurs of agreement.

The gingerbeer glass was soothingly cold and Lyle rolled it across his forehead, from one side to the other, slowly, to and fro. When the glass was warm he drank the gingerbeer. But it was then too sweet and he couldn't finish it. His hands grew steadily stickier; he was embarrassed to put the glass down.

There was a movement, a stir, groups forming and reforming, higher, sharper laughter from all; and then most of the people were gone.

Those who remained became involved in an argument in the center of the room. Anna was protesting, "Oh, we can't now. We're going to eat soon. What about this afternoon?"

"Rubbish. It's early. You're not going to have it hot anyway. So come along. If the kids get hungry there's masses at our place. They'll eat again, don't you worry."

"No really, I don't think so," Anna said. "Look how many there are of us. What about you, John?" She addressed her husband.

"I'm easy. Just say the word." He was a big man and his face was red from the morning's steady drinking. He was grinning happily, content to let others settle it all. So long as there was another drink, somewhere, soon.

The woman who earlier had been in the kitchen with Anna said, "Nonsense, you're all coming. It's your turn to sit down for a while."

"Oh well, all right. Only for an hour."

"Let's go."

Anna said. "You'd better comb your hair a bit, Lyle. You've been rubbing it."

He said, "Would you mind if I went for a walk or something or sat on the verandah until you come back?"

"Don't you want to go? We're all going."

"I've got a headache."

2 **to omit** to leave out – 4 **solemn** ['sɒləm] – **to address** [-'-] to speak to – 7 **soothing** comforting – 12 **stir** *here:* excited movement – 14 **to be involved in s.th.** to take part in s.th. – **argument** quarrel, discussion – 23 **content** [-'-] happily satisfied

"Oh, dear," Anna said.

"It doesn't matter, you can lock up," Lyle said. "I can stay on the verandah."

"No, it's all right. Minnie's got to stay here and clean up anyway," Anna said, and then looked thoughtful, as if reassessing her decision.

"Isn't he coming?" the other woman asked.

"No," Anna said. "He's got a headache."

"Oh," the woman said. "Oh," and she looked at Anna.

"Minnie's going to be here," Anna said again, reassuring herself.

They left without further questions, and Lyle listened to the sounds of their departure. He stood around listlessly.

The Malay woman was cleaning up the mess in the lounge, stacking glasses and clearing ashtrays. He stood in the doorway watching her but she paid no attention and when she had finished straightening the cushions and drawing the curtains against the heat she pressed silently past him and went out into the backyard to her room. He heard its door slam distantly. She would probably sleep until called to serve dinner.

He felt a sudden uneasiness about being left alone like this. The house was alarmingly empty, though still filled with its Christmas spice. He now fervently wished he had gone with them. His next regret was that he had come at all, the loneliness in the mess and the dormitories at least was familiar.

In the dining room the great array of prepared food lay pensive under the cheesecloths spread to keep off the flies. It was a sumptuous silence here, and over it now and then there flicked a flash of complementary color from the balloons on the ceiling as they caught some brief light when the curtains stirred from the merest breath outside. The salads – potato with grated pineapple, orange, crayfish and avocado, egg, papaya, and so many more – stood deep and undisturbed in their bowls, around vases crammed with proteas, roses, and chrysan-

5 **to reassess** to rethink – 11 **listless** without energy or enthusiasm – 12 **to stack** to pile up – 17 **to slam** to shut (a door) with a bang – 21 **spice** *here:* aromatic smell of cinnamon, ginger, etc. – **fervent** intense – 22 **mess** *here:* dining-room – 23 **dormitory** room where several people sleep – 24 **array** [-'-] display – **pensive** quiet and thoughtful – 25 **sumptuous** *(lit.)* magnificent – 29 **grated** rubbed into small pieces – **crayfish** *Languste* – 31 **protea** South African bush with big flowers

themums. There were cold turkeys, a suckling pig, sliced ham, duckling, various jellied meats, sweets, candied watermelon, fruits, raisins, nuts. There were Christmas crackers, paper hats, and tall new candles. Lyle had never seen anything like it. He wanted to pick something up, a nut, a sweet, and to eat it and break this spell of unreal anticipation, to convince himself of its intended gaiety. But he was afraid. He couldn't.

He wandered onto the verandah and the light there was so fierce by this time that it blinded him and set his head throbbing violently again.

Below the verandah the houses fell toward Table Bay in a dazzling avalanche of whitewash and red tile. Out beyond the whaleback hump of Robben Island in the center of the bay the sun hammered silver from the sea. You could see the long shadowed creases of the South Atlantic swell moving in with slow appraisal of the shore, searching where to break.

There was no movement in the harbor below, no tug adrift; two Union-Castle mailships stood dozing in their elegant dress of lavender and red and black, lending a tone that seemed specially festive for the day. A big whale factory ship lay between them.

The only person was a Cape Colored, who sat on the edge of the pavement near the front of the house, his head sunk upon his arms, lost in thought or sleep.

Then a double-decker bus came by, half-empty, and two blond boys a little older than Lyle got off. They were in khaki shorts and carried their bathing suits wrapped in towels. Their hair was still wet from the sea. A woman simultaneously appeared on the verandah of a house up the road, summoned no doubt by the sound of the bus, and she beckoned. "We're waiting," she called cheerfully, and the boys broke into a run and disappeared inside.

1 **suckling pig** baby pig *(Spanferkel)* – 2 **jellied meat** *Sülze* – 3 **Christmas crackers** a little surprise wrapped up in paper, to be opened by pulling *(Knallbonbon)* – 5 **spell** short period of time; magic charm – **anticipation** [ˌ---ˈ--] act of looking forward to s.th. – 6 **gaiety** [ˈgeɪətɪ] joyfulness – 8 **to throb** to beat painfully – 9 **Table Bay** north of Capetown – **dazzling** brilliant, very bright – 10 **avalanche** [ˈævəlɑːnʃ] *Lawine* – **whitewash** *Kalkanstrich* – **tile** [aɪ] material used for roofs – 11 **hump** small hill; lump – 12 **crease** fold – 13 **swell** *here:* the regular movement of waves – **appraisal** consideration, observation – 15 **tug** tug-boat *(Schlepper)* – **adrift** *here:* moving on the sea – 16 **to doze** to be half asleep – 18 **factory ship** a ship where fish products are made as soon as the fish are caught – 19 **Cape Colored** mixed blood descendants of the Hottentots, the original inhabitants of the region near the Cape of Good Hope – 26 **to beckon** to make a sign to s.o. to come

Lyle and the Cape Colored once more were the only ones left adrift amongst these dense, preoccupied suburban houses.

The street was quite empty, and so was the road that traversed the sun-burned expanse of Green Point common far below, near the docks. Later, when they had slept the insensible sleep of summer heat and heavy dinner, the rush of secondary gift-giving would start in the city and the motorists would pass down there, and up here, in a fast and steady stream, renewing the morning's rounds of visits. But only later. Now there was this hush of Christmas noon, heavier than any Sunday; a hush of heat and unblemished sky which he somberly considered while the silence of the house behind him itself grew deeper. But there was no solace in this stillness and its blue-white beauty. He felt only a great sense of absence, himself from somewhere: the only man outside the caves, beyond the feast.

For the first time that day Lyle wondered about his parents and some other Christmas that might have been his; felt for that moment as though he had been misdirected, that there was indeed another Christmas that was his, that they were waiting for him as that woman had been waiting for her sons. But the day seemed to grow only more still and indrawn, absolute in its emptiness and clarity, and himself more desolately observant of these.

There was a flare of gramophone music from somewhere, swiftly reduced. Laughter.

Lyle rose and then, from some compulsion, went out onto the street and up to the colored man. He touched him on the shoulder and the man looked up quickly. His eyes were alert, as though he had anticipated the approach and expected some sort of interference with his meditation.

"Hello," Lyle said.

"Hello," the man said. He was young. About twenty. He looked at Lyle steadily.

2 **dense** close together – **preoccupied** to be lost in one's own thoughts – 4 **expanse** [-'-] wide area – **common** *here:* a kind of public park – 5 **insensible** unable to feel anything – 9 **hush** silence, peacefulness – 10 **unblemished** clear, faultless – **somber** ['sɒmbə] (*BE* **sombre**) serious, sad – 12 **solace** ['--] feeling of comfort – 21 **desolate** lonely and depressed – **observant** able to notice things – 22 **flare** *here:* sudden noise – **swiftly** quickly – 24 **compulsion** uncontrolled desire to do s.th. – 26 **alert** [-'-] wide awake, paying full attention – **to anticipate** [æn'tɪsɪpeɪt] to feel or know in advance

"I thought something might be the matter," Lyle said.

"Oh," the man said, and his expression relaxed. "I sat down and I fell asleep." He yawned. "What's the time?"

"Going on for one."

"Christ," the man said. "I should've been aboard ship by now. We sail at three, and I've missed my dinner." He shook his head. "Jong, I've had a lot to drink. I've got a terrible hangover. I started walking from Hout Bay when the sun came up. I didn't even have my bus fare left. That's a long way to walk. How many miles?"

"Dunno."

"I'd say seven."

"I don't know how far it is."

"Aren't you having Christmas?"

"Yes," Lyle said.

"Do you live here?"

"I've just come for the day."

"Where?"

"There."

"Other people there?"

"They've all gone out."

"Can you do me a favor then?"

"I'll try. What's it?"

"Get me a drink of water please, man. There's nowhere I can get a drink."

"Sure," Lyle said.

He went across to the house and found a tin mug he remembered the Malay woman using. Beside it, in a special niche above the sink, separate from the household dishes, were her plates and utensils as well. There was a Christmas cracker and a paper hat beside them today.

He carried the water back carefully and the man put it back with a single gulp.

"Ah," he said. "That was good." He frowned. "You can't go to a café or a European house for a drink because they think you've come to

3 **to yawn** *gähnen* – 6 **Jong** *(S.Afr. informal)* Boy! – 7 **hangover** the feeling one has after having drunk too much alcohol – 8 **Hout** [haʊt] **Bay** south of Capetown – 10 **dunno** *(informal)* I don't know – 26 **mug** big cup used without a saucer – 31 **put it back with a single gulp** drank it in one go

steal and they chase you or call the dogs. So what do you do? Thank you very much, that was really a favor."

"Would you like some more?"

"I would," the man said. "I really would." He rose slowly to his feet and dejectedly examined his clothes and started brushing them off with his hands. He was well dressed but the suit was crumpled and dusty. "The first time I have this suit on, look what it's like. It cost me ten quid. That's one thing I hate, man, to get kaffir drunk like that." He sighed. "Oh well, I've got lots of time to clean it."

"Where are you going?"

"Whaling. That's her down there," and he indicated the factory ship below. "When I come back in the autumn I'll have five hundred pounds. Then I'm going to Canada. I've got a girl friend there. My feeansay." He pronounced the word with an air of sophistication, took out his wallet, and flipped it open. "That's her. I'm engaged. Next Christmas this time I'll be there. Saint John, New Brunswick. We took oranges there."

"She's European," Lyle blurted.

"Yes," the man said. "So am I. Over there." It was true. He could have passed for white. His skin was olive, his hair thick and straight; only his nose was a little broad and so were his lips, but he was pleasant looking and had thick shoulders.

"Did you see snow in Canada?"

"Yes."

"Do you like it?"

"I don't like the cold, but it's nice to pass for white."

"I suppose so. There's a boy at the place where I am, at my school. He was born in England and he's seen snow."

"You couldn't fetch me that other drink of water, please?"

"Are you hungry?"

"Yes."

"Come inside," Lyle said.

"You mean in the house?"

5 **dejected** [-'--] unhappy – 8 **quid** [kwɪd] *(slang)* S.Afr. rand or pound sterling – **kaffir drunk** *(S.Afr. slang)* very drunk – 14 **feeansay** = **fiancé/fiancée** person to whom one is engaged to be married – **sophistication** refinement, experience – 15 **wallet** man's purse for money and papers – 18 **to blurt** to say s.th. suddenly and thoughtlessly

"Yes, there's no one there."

"Got any dogs?"

"No."

The man looked up and down the street. "You're sure you know what you're doing? I don't want any trouble. I want to get to my ship. What if they come back and find a colored man in the house? You're a small boy and you don't know what you're doing – I don't like going into European houses."

"They won't be back for a while," Lyle assured him. "They've just gone. I feel like dinner. Everybody's having it."

"Why didn't you go with them?" the man asked suspiciously.

Lyle shrugged.

"Come and see the dinner they've got," he said.

The colored man was awestruck by the splendor of the table. "My God," he said. "I've never seen anything like that. Not even at my brother's wedding. Man, I don't like this. It's all there waiting for them; they come in here licking their chops and they see me? ... No!"

"Don't worry," Lyle said. He felt master of the situation, proud of his own resolve against the older man's hesitation. "We'll take it off the tops of the salads and smooth it over. Don't take all your nuts or sweets from the same dish. See?" He had begun filling a plate, and he handed it to the man, who began eating slowly and then with relish. "Whose place is this?"

"My aunt's."

"Why didn't you stay at your own home?"

"I don't have one. I'm at Tokai."

The man put his plate down slowly. "You mean the reformatory?"

"Yes."

"Jesus Christ man are you lying to me?"

"About what?"

"This house. What are you doing here?"

"I just told you."

"Then why aren't you at Tokai? Did you run away?"

11 **suspiciously** with distrust – 12 **to shrug** to lift the shoulders instead of giving an answer – 14 **awestruck** very impressed – **splendor** (*BE* **splendour**) great beauty and magnificence – 17 **to lick one's chops** *(slang)* to look forward to s.th. (esp. a meal) with pleasure – 19 **resolve** determination – 22 **relish** ['--] enjoyment

"No. They let me off for the day – they're letting me out soon and they want me adjusted."

"I don't know what that word means," the man said.

"Oh, getting on with people."

"You get on with people all right. You get on very well with people."

"No, I don't," Lyle said. "I get on people's nerves."

"You don't. Not on mine. You're the first European who doesn't get on my nerves."

"I do, honestly. I get on people's nerves after a while."

"Why?"

"I do funny things."

"You do funny things all right. What sort of things?"

"Oh, all sorts. It depends. Sometimes I make noises."

"What noises?"

The man had seated himself and he was eating with increasing enjoyment, his eyes roving the table as he talked, his arm extending occasionally to filch some sweetmeat that caught his fancy. "What noises?" he repeated, looking at Lyle, who had become thoughtful.

"Oh, moans and groans, dog in agony, noises like that."

"Do you do it all the time?"

"No."

"What makes you do it?"

"I dunno, I just want to. I get a feeling I want to."

"People must think you're crazy."

"I dunno."

"What do they say?"

"Oh, nothing much. They just talk a lot afterwards and look at me. I don't do it such a lot at Tokai, except when I'm by myself, because the other boys don't like it and they put me in the shower."

"But is that what they put you in Tokai for, those noises?"

"Sort of," Lyle said, and then asked, "Do you want to pull a cracker?"

"That red one," the man said.

They pulled. "There's a paper hat inside," Lyle said. "You must put it on."

2 **to get adjusted** to get used to new circumstances – 16 **to rove** to wander about – 17 **to filch** *(informal)* to steal – **sweetmeat** *(lit.)* fine food made with sugar – 19 **moans and groans** low sounds of pain – **agony** great pain

They pulled another cracker, and then both put on their paper hats. "I'm getting full," the man said. "What did you mean, 'sort of'? What for?"

"I used to make a lot of noises when I was in the Anglican Home. I was put there after my parents went off. They used to get drunk and quarrel and then he stabbed her, and she was sick, and I don't know what happened to them after that. They were always quarreling. I didn't care when they went off. But I used to make a lot of noises then, and I was in the choir and Easter when the Bishop came for the sermon I did dog in agony in the middle of it. Then they made me polish the altar brass in the vestry and there was a hundred pounds in the collection box and I gave it to a native."

"What native?"

"He looked like a Zulu. He was very big. I leaned out the vestry window and he was passing and I gave it to him. I gave him the whole box. They said afterwards it was a hundred pounds."

"What did he say?"

"He laughed and he ran away."

"Damn right he ran. Did they catch him?"

"No. They wanted to know what the native looked like. He just looks like any native, I said. Then they put me in the reformatory."

"I was going to steal something," the man said. "But I won't."

"What?"

"This fountain pen." He took it from his pocket and placed it on the table. "I picked it up when we came in. I don't mind taking from Europeans. But never get your mates into trouble."

"No," Lyle said.

They sat in their paper hats examining the table. The room was very quiet. The dishes showed deep indentations.

"We've done a lot of damage here," the man said. "Let's clean it up quickly or you'll get into trouble." He was laughing. "That really was Christmas. That was Christmas forever for that Zulu."

"He couldn't believe it," Lyle said.

"Nor would I," the man said. "But I wouldn't wait to believe it either; I'd run like he did."

6 **to stab s.o.** to push a knife into s.o. – 11 **brass** *here:* objects made of brass *(Messing)* – **vestry** small room in a church for the priest or minister – 26 **mate** friend – 29 **indentation** *Delle*

"He ran very fast. I watched him."

They leveled the salad bowls, patted the tops into shape, dusted the table of crumbs, and Lyle took the dirty plates to the kitchen and rinsed them.

"I've got to go now," the man said. "That was the best Christmas dinner I ever had."

"Me too," Lyle said.

They went out to the verandah and down to the street. They were still wearing their paper hats and looked at one another and the man touched Lyle's shoulder. "You're a nice boy. You mustn't go on doing funny things. What's going to happen when you grow up and you still do funny things?"

"I won't anymore. Not so much." Lyle added, "I'll watch you sail. I wish I were going. I'd like to go away, on Christmas Day."

"Some day you'll go, when you're big. Ag, shame now, you mustn't cry."

"I'm not."

"Goodbye then."

He crossed the road and began running down the hill toward the docks. He turned suddenly his teeth white under his pink hat. "Merry Christmas," he shouted.

"Merry Christmas," Lyle cried. He watched the man disappear and then took off his paper hat, folded it carefully, put it in his pocket, and went back to his bench on the verandah.

2 **to pat** to tap gently with the open hand – 4 **to rinse** to clean with running water – 15 **Ag** (*S.Afr.*) pronounced as in German *Ach*

Biographical Note

Noël Mostert was born in South Africa in 1929, but went to Canada at the age of twenty. Until 1962 he worked as a correspondent for various Canadian newspapers and magazines, but since then he has lived as a freelance writer, contributing articles and stories to the New Yorker, Reader's Digest, Harper's Magazine *etc. He has also published some non-fiction, including* Supership, *a book about oil-tankers which was published in eighteen countries including Germany. His latest book,* Frontiers, *is a history of South Africa. It appeared simultaneously in New York and London in 1992.* A Christmas Dinner *first appeared in* Harper's Magazine *in December, 1964. Noël Mostert now lives in Morocco.*

Bernard Mac Laverty

A Present for Christmas

McGettigan woke in the light of midday, numb with the cold. He had forgotten to close the door the night before and his coat had slipped off him onto the boards of the floor. He swivelled round on the sofa and put the overcoat on, trying to stop shivering. At his feet there was a dark green wine bottle and his hand shook as he reached out to test its weight. He wondered if he had had the foresight to leave a drop to warm himself in the morning. It was empty and he flung it in the corner with the others, wincing at the noise of the crash.

He got to his feet and buttoned the only button on his coat. The middle section he held together with his hands thrust deep in his pockets and went out into the street putting his head down against the wind. He badly needed something to warm him.

His hand searched for his trouser pocket without the hole. There was a crumpled pound and what felt like a fair amount of silver. He was all right. Nobody had fleeced him the night before. Yesterday he had got his Christmas money from the Assistance and he had what would cure him today, with maybe something left for Christmas Day itself.

Strannix's bar was at the back of the Law Courts about two minutes from McGettigan's room but to McGettigan it seemed like an eternity. His thin coat flapped about his knees. He was so tall he always thought he got the worst of the wind. When he pushed open the door of the bar he felt the wave of heat and smoke and spirit smells surround him like a hug. He looked quickly behind the bar. Strannix wasn't on. It was only the barman, Hughie – a good sort. McGettigan went up to the counter and stood shivering. Hughie set him up a hot

1 **numb** [nʌm] stiff, paralysed – 3 **to swivel** to turn round quickly – 4 **to shiver** to tremble with cold or fear – 8 **to wince** to make a quick movement showing bodily pain – 10 **to thrust, thrust, thrust** to push quickly and forcefully – 14 **crumpled** *zerknittert* – 15 **to fleece** *here:* to rob – 16 **Assistance** = National Assistance, the old name for Social Security or Income Support – 21 **to flap** to move quickly up and down – 24 **hug** embrace

wine without a word. McGettigan put the money down on the marble slab but Hughie gestured it away.

"Happy Christmas, big lad," he said. McGettigan nodded still unable to speak. He took the steaming glass, carrying it in both hands, to a bench at the back of the bar, and waited a moment until it cooled a bit. Then he downed it in one. He felt his insides unfurl and some of the pain begin to disappear. He got another one which he paid for.

After the second the pains had almost gone and he could unbend his long legs, look up and take in his surroundings. It was past two by the bar clock and there was a fair number in the bar. Now he saw the holly and the multi-coloured decorations and the HAPPY XMAS written white on the mirror behind the bar. There was a mixture of people at the counter, locals and ones in from the Law Courts with their waistcoats and sharp suits. They were wise-cracking and laughing and talking between each other which didn't happen every day of the year. With Strannix off he could risk going up to the bar. You never know what could happen. It was the sort of day a man could easily get drink bought for him.

He stood for a long time smiling at their jokes but nobody took any notice of him so he bought himself another hot wine and went back to his seat. It was funny how he'd forgotten that it was so near Christmas. One day was very much the same as another. Long ago Christmases had been good. There had been plenty to eat and drink. A chicken, vegetables and spuds, all at the same meal, ending up with plum-duff and custard. Afterwards the Da, if he wasn't too drunk, would serve out the mulled claret. He would heat a poker until it glowed red and sparked white when bits of dust hit it as he drew it from the fire – that was another thing, they'd always had a fire at Christmas – then he'd plunge it down the neck of the bottle and serve

1 **marble slab** board of white stone on top of the counter – 2 **to gesture** ['dʒestʃə] to make a certain movement instead of talking – 3 **lad** *(dialect)* boy, young man, fellow – 6 **to down it in one** *(informal)* to drink it in one go – **to unfurl** to unfold, to unroll – 8 **to unbend** to straighten – 11 **Xmas** a short form of "Christmas", X being the first letter of the Greek word for Christ – 14 **waistcoat** ['weiskəʊt] sleeveless jacket worn under another jacket – **sharp** *(slang)* stylish – **to wise-crack** to make clever, amusing remarks – 24 **spuds** *(informal)* potatoes – 25 **plum-duff** *(informal)* Christmas pudding – **custard** *Vanillesoße* – **Da** short form of Dad(dy) – 26 **mulled claret** hot and spicy red wine – **poker** metal stick to stir the coal in a fire – 27 **to glow** to be bright and shiny with warmth – **to spark** to send out little bits of fire or light – 29 **to plunge** to push down with a quick movement

the wine out in cups with a spoonful of sugar in the bottom of each. Then they knew that they could go out and play with their new things until midnight if they liked, because the Ma and the Da would get full and fall asleep in their chairs. By bedtime their new things were always broken but it didn't seem to matter because you could always do something with them. Those were the days.

But there were bad times as well. He remembered the Christmas Day he ended lying on the cold lino, crying in the corner, sore from head to foot after a beating the Da had given him. He had knocked one of the figures from the crib on the mantlepiece and it smashed to white plaster bits on the hearth. The Da had bought the crib the day before and was a bit the worse for drink and he had laid into him with the belt – buckle and all. Even now he couldn't remember which figure it was.

McGettigan was glad he wasn't married. He could get full whenever he liked without children to worry about. He was his own master. He could have a good Christmas. He searched his pockets and took out all his money and counted it. He could afford a fair bit for Christmas Day. He knew he should get it now, just in case, and have it put to one side. Maybe he could get something to eat as well.

He went up to the counter and Hughie leaned over to hear him above the noise of the bar. When McGettigan asked him for a carry-out Hughie reminded him that it was only half-past two. Then McGettigan explained that he wanted it for Christmas. Three pint bottles of stout and three of wine.

"Will this do?" asked Hughie holding up the cheapest wine in the place and smiling. He put the bottles in a bag and left it behind the counter.

"You'll tell the boss it's for me, if he comes in," said McGettigan.

"If Strannix comes in you'll be out on your ear," Hughie said.

Strannix was a mean get and everybody knew it. He hated McGettigan, saying that he was the type of customer he could well do without. People like him got the place a bad name. What he really meant

3 **full** *(slang)* drunk – 8 **lino** ['laɪnəʊ] linoleum – **sore** aching, hurting – 10 **crib** *here:* figures representing the birth of Christ – **mantlepiece** shelf above the fireplace – 11 **plaster** *Gips* – **hearth** [hɑ:θ] fireplace – 12 **to lay into s.o.** *(informal)* to beat s.o. terribly – 13 **buckle** metal thing to fasten a belt – 22 **carry-out** *(informal)* drink that you take home from a pub – 24 **pint** [paɪnt] a measure of liquid (0,568 l.) – 25 **stout** strong dark beer – 30 **to be out on your ear** to be thrown out – 31 **mean get** *(slang)* nasty person

was that the judges and lawyers, who drank only the dearest and best – and lots of it – might object to McGettigan's sort. Strannix would strangle his grandmother for a halfpenny. It was a standing joke in the bar for the lawyers, when served with whiskey, to say, "I'll just put a little more water in this." Strannix was an out-and-out crook. He not only owned the bar but also the houses of half the surrounding streets. McGettigan paid him an exorbitant amount for his room and although he hated doing it he paid as regularly as possible because he wanted to hold onto this last shred. You were beat when you didn't have a place to go. His room was the last thing he wanted to lose.

Now that he was feeling relaxed McGettigan got himself a stout and as he went back to his seat he saw Judge Boucher come in. Everybody at the bar wished him a happy Christmas in a ragged chorus. One young lawyer having wished him all the best, turned and rolled his eyes and sniggered into his hot whiskey.

Judge Boucher was a fat man, red-faced with a network of tiny broken purple veins. He wore a thick, warm camel-hair overcoat and was peeling off a pair of fur-lined gloves. McGettigan hadn't realized he was bald the first time he had seen him because then he was wearing his judge's wig and sentencing him to three months for drunk and disorderly. McGettigan saw him now tilt his first gin and tonic so far back that the lemon slice hit his moustache. He slid the glass back to Hughie who refilled it. Judge Boucher cracked and rubbed his hands together and said something about how cold it was, then he pulled a piece of paper from his pocket and handed it to Hughie with a wad of money. The judge seemed to be buying for those around him so McGettigan went up close to him.

"How're ye Judge," he said. McGettigan was a good six inches taller than the judge, but round-shouldered. The judge turned and looked up at him.

3 **to strangle** to kill by squeezing the throat – **standing** *here:* constant, regular – 5 **out-and-out crook** complete criminal – 7 **exorbitant** [-'---] enormous – 9 **shred** fragment, little bit of s.th. – **beat** *(dialect)* beaten, finished – 13 **ragged** ['rægɪd] *here:* uneven, uncoordinated – 15 **to snigger** to laugh quietly and disrespectfully – 17 **vein** [veɪn] – 18 **to peel off** *here:* to take off – 19 **bald** [ɔ:] with no hair – 20 **wig** artificial hair – **to sentence** to say in court what the punishment will be – **disorderly** behaving in an uncontrolled and violent way – 21 **to tilt** to tip, to put in a sloping position – 22 **moustache** [mə'stɑ:ʃ] hair on upper lip – 25 **wad** [wɒd] **of money** some banknotes folded together – 26 **buying for those around him** buying a round of drinks for the whole group is a custom in British pubs

"McGettigan. Keeping out of trouble, eh?" he said.

"Yis, sur. But things is bad at the minute … like … you know how it is. Now if I had the money for a bed …" said McGettigan fingering the stubble of his chin.

"I'll buy you no drink," snapped the judge. "That's the cause of your trouble, man. You look dreadful. How long is it since you've eaten?"

"It's not the food your lordship …" began McGettigan but he was interrupted by the judge ordering him a meat pie. He took it with mumbled thanks and went back to his seat once again.

"Happy Christmas," shouted the judge across the bar.

Just then Strannix came in behind the bar. He was a huge muscular man and had his sleeves rolled up to his biceps. He talked in a loud Southern brogue. When he spied McGettigan he leaned over the bar hissing, "Ya skinney big hairpin. I thought I told you if ever I caught you …"

"Mr. Strannix," called the judge from the other end of the counter. Strannix's face changed from venom to smile as he walked the duckboards to where the judge stood.

"Yes, Judge, what can I do for you?" he said. The judge had now become the professional.

"Let him be," he said. "Good will to all men and all that." He laughed loudly and winked in McGettigan's direction. Strannix filled the judge's glass again and stood with a fixed smile waiting for the money.

At four o'clock the judge's car arrived for him and after much handshaking and backslapping he left. McGettigan knew his time had come. Strannix scowled over at him and with a vicious gesture of his big thumb, ordered him out.

"Hughie has a parcel for me," said McGettigan defiantly, "… and it's paid for," he added before Strannix could ask. Strannix grabbed the

2 **Yis, sur** *(dialect)* Yes, sir – 4 **stubble** man's rough facial hair if he has not shaved – 5 **to snap** *here:* to speak in a sharp and unfriendly way – 6 **dreadful** [e] terrible, awful – 7 **your lordship** the term used when you speak to a judge – 9 **to mumble** to speak unclearly – 13 **brogue** Irish (or Scots) accent – **to spy** *here:* to see, to catch sight of – 14 **to hiss** *here:* to speak in an angry manner – **skinney/skinny** very thin – 17 **venom** *here:* nastiness, bitterness – **duckboards** a path of boards over wet ground (*here:* behind the counter) – 22 **to wink** to shut one eye quickly as a sign – 27 **to scowl** to look in a bad-tempered way – **vicious** ['vɪʃəs] brutal – 29 **defiant** [dɪ'faɪənt] rebellious, aggressive

paper bag, then came round the counter and shoved it into McGettigan's arms and guided him firmly out the door. As the door closed McGettigan shouted, "I hope this Christmas is your last."

The door opened again and Strannix stuck his big face out. "If you don't watch yourself I'll be round for the rent," he snarled.

McGettigan spat on the pavement loud enough for Strannix to hear.

It was beginning to rain and the dark sky seemed to bring on the night more quickly. McGettigan clutched his carry-out in the crook of his arm, his exposed hand getting cold. Then he sensed something odd about the shape in the bag. There was a triangular shape in there. Not a shape he knew.

He stopped at the next street light and opened the bag. There was a bottle of whiskey, triangular in section. There was also a bottle of vodka, two bottles of gin, a bottle of brandy and what looked like some tonic.

He began to run as fast as he could. He was in bad shape, his breath rasped in his throat, his boots were filled with lead, his heart moved up and thumped in his head. As he ran he said a frantic prayer that they wouldn't catch him.

Once inside his room he set his parcel gently on the sofa, snibbed the door and lay against it panting and heaving. When he got his breath back he hunted by the yard, in the last remaining daylight, for some nails he knew were in a tin. Then he hammered them through the door into the jamb with wild swings of a hatchet. Then he pushed the sofa against the door and looked around the room. There was nothing else that could be moved. He sat down on the floor against the wall at the window and lined the bottles in front of him. Taking them out they tinkled like full bells. In silence he waited for Strannix.

Within minutes he came, he and Judge Boucher stamping into the hallway. They battered on the door, shouting his name. Strannix

1 **to shove** [ʃʌv] to push hard – 5 **to snarl** [snɑːl] to speak in a fierce, angry voice – 6 **to spit, spat, spat** *spucken* – 8 **to clutch** to hold tightly – **crook** *here:* curve of his bent arm – 9 **to sense** to feel (in one's mind) –10 **triangular** [traɪˈæŋgjʊlə] three-cornered – 16 **in bad shape** not physically fit – 17 **to rasp** to make a rough, scraping noise – **lead** [led] *Blei* – 18 **to thump** to beat hard – **frantic** quick and desperate – 20 **to snib** to lock from the inside – 21 **to pant** to breathe quickly and loudly – **to heave** *here:* to gasp for breath – 22 **to hunt** *here:* to search – 24 **jamb** [dʒæm] frame of a door – **hatchet** small axe – 28 **to tinkle** to make a sound like a bell – 29 **to stamp** to walk heavily – 30 **to batter** to hit very hard

shouted, "McGettigan. We know you're in there. If you don't come out I'll kill you."

The judge's voice tried to reason. "I bought you a meat pie, McGettigan." He sounded genuinely hurt.

But his voice was drowned by Strannix.

"McGettigan, I know you can hear me. If you don't hand back that parcel I'll get you evicted." There was silence. Low voices conferred outside the door. Then Strannix shouted again. "Evicted means put out, you stupid hairpin."

Then after some more shouting and pummelling on the door they went away, their mumbles and footsteps fading gradually.

McGettigan laughed as he hadn't laughed for years, his head thrown back against the wall. He played eeny-meeny-miney-mo with the bottles in front of him – and the whiskey won. The click of the metal seal breaking he thought much nicer than the pop of a cork. He teased himself by not drinking immediately but got up and, to celebrate, put a shilling in the meter to light the gas fire. Its white clay sections were broken and had all fallen to the bottom. The fire banged loudly because it had not been lit for such a long time, making him jump back and laugh.

Then McGettigan pulled the sofa up to the fire and kicked off his boots. His toes showed white through the holes in his socks and the steam began to rise from his feet. A rectangle of light fell on the floor from the streetlamp outside the uncurtained window. The whiskey was red and gold in the light from the gas fire.

He put the bottle to his head and drank. The heat from inside him met the warmth of his feet and they joined in comfort. Again and again he put the bottle to his head and each time he lowered it he listened to the music of the back-slop. Soon the window became a bright diamond and he wondered if it was silver rain drifting in the halo of the

3 **to reason** to argue – 4 **genuine** ['dʒenjʊɪn] true, real – 5 **to drown** *here: übertönen* – 7 **to evict** [-'-] to make s.o. leave his house or flat – **to confer** [-'-] to talk and discuss – 10 **to pummel** to beat continuously – 11 **to fade** to become weaker – 13 **eeny-meeny...** children's counting rhyme – 15 **seal** *here:* tight-fitting metal top – 16 **to tease** *necken* – 17 **meter** instrument to measure the amount of gas that is used – 23 **rectangle** shape with four sides – 29 **back-slop** *here:* noise of liquid as it returns to the bottom of the bottle or container – 30 **halo** circle of light often painted around the head of Christ or saints

lamp or if it was snow for Christmas. Choirs of boy sopranos sang carols and McGettigan, humming, conducted slowly with his free hand and the room bloomed in the darkness of December

2 **to conduct** [-'-] *here:* to beat the rhythm for a choir or orchestra – 3 **to bloom** *here:* to become bright and beautiful like a flower

Biographical Note

Bernard Mac Laverty, novelist and short-story writer, was born in Belfast, Northern Ireland, in 1942. He studied English as a mature student, afterwards qualifying as a teacher. He left Ireland in the early 1970s to live on Islay, off the west coast of Scotland. His breakthrough came in 1977 with a collection of short stories (Secrets and Other Stories) *which won an award, as did the novel* Lamb *in 1980. Both* Lamb *and* Cal *(1983), a love story set against the background of the troubles in Northern Ireland, have been made into successful films.*

Mac Laverty's characters – young boys, priests, drunkards, lonely people or people in difficult situations – are often caught at moments of sudden knowledge, the Joycean 'epiphany'. His style is poignant, clear-cut and simple. As a short-story writer he is widely esteemed as "one of the best practitioners of the genre" (New Statesman).

Bernard Mac Laverty now lives in Glasgow.

Martha Brooks

Waiting for the Carollers

My parents called me Naomi because they both liked the name. I think that's the last thing they ever agreed on.

December twenty-first, I got on a jet plane heading west, with a stopover in Calgary. My destination: Kelowna, British Columbia, because that's where my grandmother lives. Her daughter, that's my mother, saw me off at the airport. Dad couldn't come because of a business meeting, he said. I know it's because he wasn't in total agreement with my going.

I wasn't in total agreement with my going.

Christmas can be a real bummer for some people. I know the ads all tell you how it's terrific and everything. But people starve to death at Christmas. Bombs go off. Countries are overthrown. Sick people get sicker and die. Some healthy people take guns and shoot themselves. Others feel disappointed because they didn't get what they wanted, or the family get-together was messed up by everyone fighting, or somebody got drunk, or somebody got really sick with the flu, or all of the above.

Christmas, for me, has never been an especially joyous occasion. I mean, what's left after they've told you there isn't a Santa Claus?

I'll bet even Jesus Christ Himself was sometimes depressed at Christmas.

My grandmother is retired. Grandpa died three years ago. Grandma makes pottery in the winter. In summer she sells peaches from her peach trees. When I say she's retired I mean that my grandparents moved to Kelowna when he retired so that makes Grandma sort of retired too.

carollers a group of people who sing Christmas songs (carols) – 1 **Naomi** [neɪ'əʊmɪ/ 'neɪəmɪ] – 4 **Calgary** ['---] town in Alberta, Canada – **Kelowna** [kə'ləʊnə] holiday resort in British Columbia – 6 **to see s.o. off** to accompany s.o. to the station or airport – 10 **bummer** *(slang)* s.th. very unpleasant – **ad** advertisement – 15 **get-together** reunion, party – **to mess up** to spoil – 16 **flu** *(informal)* influenza *(Grippe)* – 23 **pottery** *Töpferei, Keramik*

No wonder Mom and Dad have never really gotten along. They met coming from opposite directions. Mom's dad was a zoology professor who spent his spare time fighting for world peace. Dad's dad worked for an insurance company and spent his spare time trying to improve his golf score.

Mom and Dad each came to their marriage expecting certain things. For one: that life together would be the happy idealized version each had of their own childhood home lives. They still expect it. They seem moronically unable to learn that you can't expect one person to give you all the things you want and need. Sometimes you just have to make do. God knows, I'm always making do. I don't get what I need, forget about what I might want.

I've learned that wanting is wishing your best friend would stop borrowing your clothes and never returning them. Or that you had more talent at something you work very hard at, when somebody else has talent to burn and lets it lay waste.

Needing is a different thing altogether. It's wishing for love with pennies at a dried-up well. Or waiting for family peace when home is an endless war zone.

My sister Sally says Mom and Dad will never change and she's just had to come to terms with that so why can't I. It's all very well for her to talk. Fact: she came to terms four years ago (at the ripe old age of nineteen) by getting married and moving out.

My brother Victor, who's older than Sally, remembers a time when Mom and Dad liked each other – or seemed to – and actually made jokes about how little they have in common. By the time I came along I guess it wasn't a joke anymore. I was one of the jokes they couldn't joke about.

Anyway, Mom's shipped me off to Grandma's for a boring festive season. She and Dad'll stay home and fight without me. I'm supposedly Grandma's Christmas present. Her *Christmas present,* can you believe it? I should have gotten off the plane wearing a goddamn bow around my neck.

4 **spare time** free time – 5 **golf score** number of times you hit the ball during the course of a game – 9 **moronical/moronic** *(informal)* stupid, idiotic – 11 **to make do** to put up with s.th. – 16 **talent to burn** *(informal)* a great deal of talent – to **lay waste/to go to waste** to remain unused – 22 **to come to terms with s.th.** *sich mit etwas abfinden* – 32 **goddam** *(AE slang)* damned – **bow** [bəʊ]

I have to explain about my grandmother. She's seventy-five, short, rosy, and healthy (on account of she walks six miles every day whether or not she feels like it), goes to church regularly, is an NDPer (a bloody communist, Dad says) and *she does not live alone!* She's "Living in Sin" (Dad's expression) with a man who's four years younger than her. Edgar LaChance is his name.

Good old take-a-chance Edgar has a wife who, Grandma says, is in practically a vegetable state in a Kelowna nursing home. He visits her every Tuesday and likely lies about how swell everything is back home. Not that she cares, since she's a vegetable. He could tell her the entire West Coast was slowly sinking into the Pacific Ocean and she'd probably just lie there and drool.

Grandma lives on the other side of the lake from town, part way up what everybody here calls a mountain. For somebody who's supposedly a communist, she lives pretty well. The house overlooks the orchard (you can get a lot of peach trees onto one and half acres of land) and is all natural cedar with a huge fireplace smack dab in the middle. The mantlepiece is about a foot thick and this morning Grandma set Edgar and me to the job of decorating it, while she rushed off to find a freshly killed turkey as she refuses to buy a frozen one at the grocery store. They're shot clear through with chemicals, she says.

This afternoon, being Tuesday – can you believe this? – we are all going over to the nursing home to have a pre-Christmas celebration with Edgar's wife. I can't imagine anything more festive and jolly than that.

I'm even supposed to take her a present. Grandma bought Lily-of-the-Valley bath salts for me to take. I don't know how Edgar is going to introduce me. Am I the granddaughter of the woman he's living with? Who is his friend? Or his next-door neighbour? I don't even

3 **NDP** New Democratic Party, representing moderately socialist views – 4 **to live in sin** to live together with someone without being married – 8 **vegetable** *(informal) here:* s.o. whose brain has been damaged (owing to disease or old age) and who therefore merely functions or "vegetates" – 9 **swell** *(AE informal)* wonderful – 12 **to drool** to dribble at the mouth – 17 **smack dab** *(informal)* exactly, right – 21 **to be shot through with s.th.** to contain a lot of s.th. – 27 **lily-of-the-valley** *Maiglöckchen*

know if this old lady has met my grandmother. I also have a hard time visualizing how a vegetable relates to people. Does she blink her eyes once for yes, twice for no?

Edgar and I lay cedar boughs on the mantlepiece. From a kicked-around looking cardboard box he eases out a Nativity scene, an old plastic crèche all in one piece with an electric cord dangling down the back. It's exactly the kind of gaudy thing a little kid would pick out to give to somebody special at Christmas. Plastic. My grandmother has always hated plastic. Once when I came to visit, she threw out my blue and pink barrettes and bought me brown ones that I didn't like as much. "But these are plastic too," I said.

"Tortoise-shell," she corrected me, even though she knew perfectly well they were plain old plastic.

Edgar's hands are dry as leaves. The backs are spotty with age marks and his veins are raised and ropey. He places the crèche at one end of the mantlepiece. Carefully he arranges cedar around it, then plugs it in. The little bulb inside comes on and lights up the Nativity scene. I choose that moment to ask what's wrong with his wife.

"Many things," he says, not taking his eyes off the crèche. He has a slight French accent.

I patiently wait for him to elaborate.

But Edgar isn't exactly a talker. In this he is unlike my grandmother who, when she opens her mouth, doesn't close it for a long time. Edgar watches her face whenever she talks, reviews it like it's a map: her eyebrows, eyes, nose, mouth, chin, and back on up again. Carefully he watches and, at the same time, seems to be thinking his own thoughts. He listens to CBC all the time and gets the same kind of look when he lifts his head from whatever he's doing to listen to certain passages of classical music.

My grandmother returns from shopping, her arms loaded with groceries she didn't intend to buy. Edgar takes them from her, sets

2 **to blink** to open and shut the eyes quickly – 4 **bough** [baʊ] branch of a tree – 5 **to ease out** to take out carefully – **Nativity scene** picture or figures representing the Birth of Christ – 6 **crèche** *(French/AE) Krippe* – 7 **gaudy** ['gɔːdɪ] very brightly coloured – 10 **barrette** *(AE)* clasp to hold a girl's hair – 12 **tortoise-shell** *Schildpatt* – 14 **age marks** brown spots which appear in old age – 15 **ropey** like string or rope – 16 **to plug in** to switch on – 21 **to elaborate** *here:* to give more details – 27 **CBC** Canadian Broadcasting Corporation – 31 **groceries** *Lebensmittel*

them down in the kitchen. She removes her coat and hiking boots and pats her hair, which is always falling out of a loose French twist.

Edgar and I unload a few groceries. I toss a litre of Pecan Crunch ice cream into the freezer and, being in close proximity to freshly baked butter tarts, nip off the side of one and sneak it into my mouth.

"Not a fair test, one little piece," says Edgar, suddenly appearing at my shoulder. "Isn't it your duty, Naomi, to sweeten your tongue with the whole thing?"

Sweet filling encased in rich, salty pastry. Wiping away tell-tale crumbs, I follow Edgar into the living room, where Grandma stands looking at the crèche.

"You found the turkey," says Edgar, kissing her cheek.

She nods. "They were dreadfully expensive, though. Oh Edgar!" she says, enraptured. "The crèche looks beautiful!"

I can't believe I'm hearing this.

She leans her head back against his green cardigan sweater. Cashmere. Edgar's a retired business executive from Montreal.

The thought has never before occurred to me, but I guess old people can fall in love. In all this time I've never seen her look peaceful. Happy, yes. Active. Excited. In charge. But never peaceful, like now.

It's a nice moment, just standing around beside them admiring that plastic crèche. Then my grandmother breaks the mood. She sets her shoulders, pushes up her sleeves, and says, "Well, let's have lunch. Then we'll go see Vivienne."

The first thing I notice about the nursing home is that it smells depressingly of baby powder. Next thing, that practically everybody there is in a wheelchair. A bunch of old people, all lined up in the big lounge off the rotunda. Like they're waiting for something. Nurses aides in pale blue uniforms keep wheeling more old people into the lounge. The lady at the front desk tells us that a choir is arriving soon to sing Christmas carols.

2 **to pat** to touch gently with the open hand – **French twist** or **French roll** special kind of hairstyle pulled back from the face – 3 **pecan** American kind of walnut – 4 **in close proximity to** very near – 5 **to nip off** *here:* to break off – **to sneak** *here:* to put in secretly – 9 **encased in** surrounded by – **tell-tale** giving away a secret – 14 **enraptured** *(lit.)* delighted – 17 **Montreal** [ˌmɒntrɪˈɔːl] city in Quebec – 20 **in charge** in control of things, organizing s.th. – 27 **wheelchair** chair on wheels for people unable to walk – 28 **rotunda** round room, often with a dome – **aide** helper, assistant

One of the walking residents is shuffling around holding a looped-over leather belt up to his mouth. One hand is in his pocket. He stops, turns to the wall, rocks back on his heels, and talks to his belt as if it's a microphone. He makes several announcements, loudly, importantly, in Ukrainian. The others pay him no notice. Like he's normal, for God's sake.

I want to turn around and walk back out. I've never felt so depressed in all my life.

Edgar says softly, "There's Vivienne."

I don't know what I expected Vivienne to look like. I guess totally grotesque. So I'm unprepared for this beautiful old lady. Her fluffy white hair is piled on her head. She's very European-looking. She wears art-type dangling earrings that must have been custom-designed for her. Her eyes are large, soft, greenish-blue. She has long, elegant fingers; the nails are short, unpolished and perfectly groomed, as if someone has done them for her.

"She used to be an artist," Grandma whispers to me. "She was famous, in a relative way. Their daughter died when she was quite young."

When who was young? Vivienne? The daughter?

Edgar crouches beside her wheelchair. He takes her hand and says something in French. She looks at his hand holding hers. He introduces us. I'm too busy watching her face to concentrate on what he's saying. It's the strangest face – beautiful, yes, but with no expression. No recognition.

Edgar hurries to the back of the room and returns with three metal fold-up chairs. He sets them down and then we all take seats, around Vivienne. From his breast pocket Edgar removes a small leather case, unzips it, and folds it out flat on the little table affair that is attached to the arms of the wheelchair. It's a manicure set. He begins to do Vivienne's nails, all the time talking to her, sometimes in French, sometimes in English. He tells her little jokes. He chuckles and smiles, all the while gently filing away at her pink perfect nails.

1 **resident** ['---] inhabitant – **to shuffle** to walk without lifting one's feet properly – **to loop** *eine Schleife machen* – 3 **to rock** to move slowly backwards or forwards – 11 **fluffy** soft and furry – 13 **to dangle** to hang or swing loosely – **custom-designed** specially made – 15 **groomed** looked after, neat – 21 **to crouch** [kraʊtʃ] to bend down, to sit on your heels – 25 **recognition** from **to recognize** – 29 **table affair** *(informal)* a thing like a table – 32 **to chuckle** to laugh quietly

In ten minutes he says more than I've heard him say in the two days I've known him. My grandmother sits with her hands folded in her lap, saying nothing.

I guess people do what they have to do to get by. But Edgar amazes me. He does it so well, as if it hardly causes him any pain at all to be here in this place with his strange beautiful wife who was once an artist. Filing her nails is all that is left of their life together. Yet he does it with the greatest amount of love.

I feel my grandmother's hand along the back of my neck. Slowly, rhythmically, she begins to play with my hair. We sit in silence and wait for the carollers.

4 **to get by** to succeed in surviving, to manage

Biographical Note

Martha Brooks is a Canadian playwright, novelist and writer of short stories. She was born and raised in a tuberculosis sanatorium near Ninette, Manitoba, where her father was the chief surgeon. She began writing in the seventies after the birth of her daughter. She describes her subject matter as "that of initiation in the face of love and loss". This is often seen from a teenage point of view in her books, and her first award-winning novel, A Hill for Looking *(1982), is based on one year of her own childhood. Other recent publications include* Only a Paper Moon *and* Two Moons in August, *both of which appeared in 1991. Martha Brooks now lives in Winnipeg and teaches creative writing in Manitoba schools.*

"Waiting for the Carollers" *is taken from her collection* Paradise Café and Other Stories *(1988).*

Edwin Morgan

The Computer's First Christmas Card

```
j o l l y m e r r y
h o l l y b e r r y
j o l l y b e r r y
m e r r y h o l l y
h a p p y j o l l y
j o l l y j e l l y
j e l l y b e l l y
b e l l y m e r r y
h o l l y h e p p y
j o l l y M o l l y
m a r r y J e r r y
m e r r y H a r r y
h o p p y B a r r y
h e p p y J a r r y
b o p p y h e p p y
b e r r y j o r r y
j o r r y j o l l y
m o p p y j e l l y
M o l l y m e r r y
J e r r y j o l l y
b e l l y b o p p y
j o r r y h o p p y
h o l l y m o p p y
B a r r y m e r r y
J a r r y h a p p y
h a p p y b o p p y
b o p p y j o l l y
j o l l y m e r r y
m e r r y m e r r y
m e r r y m e r r y
m e r r y C h r i s
a m m e r r y a s a
C h r i s m e r r y
a s M E R R Y C H R
Y S A N T H E M U M
```

Biographical Note

Edwin Morgan, born 1920, is a Scottish poet, translator and literary critic. He was born in Glasgow, where he later studied and became Professor of English (1975–80). He has published several collections of poems including A Second Life *(1968),* Sonnets from Scotland *(1984) and* You: Anti-War Poetry *(1991). His* Collected Poems *appeared in 1990. He has also translated poetry from several languages into Scots and English, especially from the Italian. At once Scottish and European, he is committed to a stylistic pluralism which includes concrete poetry, sound poetry and playful experiment such as "The Computer's First Christmas Card", one of a series of very witty computer poems. According to one modern critic, his work is "a stimulus in many a classroom" all over Britain.*

Acknowledgements

"Christmas Morning" is reprinted from *The Stories of Frank O'Connor*, 1953. Reprinted by permission of the Peters Fraser & Dunlop Group Ltd.

"Christmas to Me Was Snow" is reprinted by permission of Mirror Syndication International.

"Merry Christmas to All" is reprinted from *One Touch of Nature and Other Stories* by B. J. Chute, published by E. P. Dutton & Co. Copyright renewed 1993 by Elizabeth Roach. Reprinted by permission of Elizabeth Roach.

"O Come Little Children" is reprinted from *Spirits of Christmas – Twenty Other-Worldly Tales*, ed. Cramer and Hartwell, Wynwood Press, New York, 1989 by permission of the author. Copyright © 1990 by Chet Williamson.

"The Nativity" is reproduced by permission of Curtis Brown, London. Copyright © 1964 by C. S. Lewis Pte Ltd.

"A Christmas Dinner" is reprinted by permission of the author. Copyright Noël Mostert, 1964.

"A Present for Christmas" is reprinted from *Secrets and Other Stories* by Bernard Mac Laverty, Jonathan Cape, 1977, by permission of Random House UK Limited.
Copyright Bernard Mac Laverty 1977.

"Waiting for the Carollers" by Martha Brooks from *Paradise Café and Other Stories*, Thistledown Press Ltd., 1988, is reprinted with permission.

"The Computer's First Christmas Card" is reprinted from *Collected Poems* by Edwin Morgan, Carcanet Press Ltd., 1990, by permission of the author.

Nicht nur für Heiligabend:

We wish you a merry Christmas and other songs

So kommt festliche Stimmung ins Klassenzimmer. Unterschiedliche Chöre und Sänger, z.B. der Mormon Tabernacle Choir oder der Choir of King's College singen 15 der bekanntesten und beliebtesten Weihnachtslieder. Da können sich Ihre Schülerinnen und Schüler einfach einmal zurücklehnen und zuhören. Es kann natürlich auch mitgesungen werden, denn alle Liedtexte sind auf der Cassetten-Beilage abgedruckt.

Cassette, 44 min. **50666**

Klett

Ernst Klett Schulbuchverlag
Postfach 10 60 16, 70049 Stuttgart

Das muß man gehört haben

Brian D. Barnes „spielt" A Christmas Carol

Für seine eigenen Lesungen hat Charles Dickens seine berühmte Weihnachtsgeschichte gestrafft. In Brian D. Barnes, der mit seinen *One Man Theatre*-Auftritten in der ganzen Welt Begeisterung auslöst, hat Dickens einen würdigen Nachfolger gefunden. Das Textbuch ist bei gleichzeitigem Einsatz der Cassette ab Klasse 10 geeignet.

Cassette, 72 min **57752**

Text, 40 Seiten **57751**

A Christmas Carol gibt es auch gekürzt und vereinfacht als *Easy Reader* und ist in dieser Fassung bereits ab Klasse 9 einsetzbar.

109 Seiten **53635**

Ernst Klett Schulbuchverlag
Postfach 10 60 16, 70049 Stuttgart